IRON BONES

THOMAS EMSON

Carrion Publishing

Also by Thomas Emson

MANEATER
SKARLET
ZOMBIE BRITANNICA
PREY
KRIMSON
PARIAH
PANDEMONIUM ROAD
KARDINAL
THE TREES AND OTHER STORIES
HOW TO WRITE A NOVEL IN 6 MONTHS (NON-FICTION)

IRONBONES

Published by Carrion Publishing

For information visit carrionpublishing.com

Book and Cover design by Blck&Grey

Cover image: Shutterstock

ISBN: 978-0-9570365-7-4

"I write fiction for lots of reasons. One is power. I'm in charge when I write. So are you. You create the world of the story. You make the rules."

Gail Carson Levine, Writing Magic: Creating Stories That Fly

I have love in me the likes of which you can scarcely imagine and rage the likes of which you would not believe. If I cannot satisfy the one, I will indulge the other.

Mary Shelley, Frankenstein

NUMBER ONE FAN

JANE COOPER HAD A face on her like she'd been told a joke she couldn't understand. Curled up on her couch, she was reading the book she'd bought three hours previously at a special midnight opening of Waterstones.

The forty-two-year-old spinster was in a world of her own. Or the world of Ironbones: The Last Dance, Kaz Payne's tenth and final novel about the eponymous superhuman serial killer.

It was 4:00 am, October 31—Halloween.

The only light came from a reading lamp on the small foot stool next to Jane's couch, which was older than her, full of holes, and reeked of cat piss. Music thumped from the flat upstairs; had done since Jane had got home three-and-a-half hours previously and started to read.

But she didn't care. The book was all that mattered. The words, as she turned the pages. Kaz Payne's words. Words Jane had devoured for more than a decade. Words that had kept her sane, kept her alive, given her hope. Words that were about to come to an end.

She shuddered at the prospect, and tears filled her eyes as she got ready to read the last few pages.

You can't kill love, she thought, you just can't.

She was filled with dread...

A decade of horror and pain was finally coming to an end for Detective Inspector Gabriel Messenger.

There was no escape this time. He wouldn't allow it.

The years he'd spent hunting Ironbones had taken their toll. Friends dead. Family dead. Ambitions dead.

The rage simmered in his chest.

Often, he'd wondered if he'd lost a little of his sanity during this pursuit. His former bosses had thought so. They had ordered him to see psychiatrists. But Messenger always found an excuse not to go. And senior officers did no more than berate him. Until they had enough and kicked him off the force.

He was once a top cop. A star; the celebrity detective who, for nearly a decade, had been pursuing the most terrifying psychopath in history—a mythic monster many argued wasn't real.

That was how some tabloids described Ironbones—monster; evil; demon—and Messenger couldn't disagree.

But he knew it was much worse than that—much worse than what the public knew.

He'd seen the monster's work up close and personal. The truly bad stuff was mostly kept out of the media. It would fuck up people's heads if they knew.

It had probably fucked up Messenger's.

Ten years ago he'd been an ambitious young detective sergeant, the future of the Metropolitan Police, many said. Media savvy. Politically astute. Pretty wife. Cute kids.

He was marked as a future Commissioner of the London force, the most senior job in British policing.

But then came Ironbones.

A killer from hell.

Seven-feet two-inches. Lethal and uncompromising. And as well as being enormous and powerful, some said he was also supernatural.

And Messenger had come to believe that over the years. He'd lost count of the times he thought he'd killed Ironbones. But the bastard just rose from the dead, over and over.

And he'd go back to what he did best—butchery.

No one was safe. Not even Messenger's kids.

The grief nearly finished him. He spiralled out of control, turned to drink. His marriage fell apart.

But what doesn't kill you makes you crazier.

And the copper came back mad. He came back cruel. He came back a monster himself.

His bosses pulled the plug: You're out, Messenger.

But Ironbones was on the rampage again. Already thirty dead. The streets awash with blood. England cowering. And there was only one man for the job.

Gabriel Messenger.

You send a man used to fighting demons to fight a demon, surely: It's not official, Messenger, this is off the books.

And here we are, he thought. I've got you at last.

Messenger was soaked through. The rain pelted down. He shivered but didn't really feel the cold. It was probably adrenalin.

He stared up the slope of the Welsh slate mountain.

Moonlight streaked the fine-grained rock, which glistened in the rain—wet, slippery, precarious.

Messenger shut his eyes and listened. The rain hammered. The wind wailed. And the beast roared.

"You can't kill me, Messenger," came the furious cry.

It was in the distance, echoing across the hillsides—but however far, that voice had the power to chill the blood.

The ex-cop listened hard, enjoying the slight hint of fear that he was certain he could hear in Ironbones's voice.

Metal rattled. The beast was caged, trying to escape.

But not this time. This time Messenger had planned everything. This time he had used every single bit of information he had gathered about Ironbones over the years to finally trap him—and he would at last put a stop to the bloodshed, to the madness.

He knew Ironbones better than he knew himself.

And the opposite was probably true.

It was almost as if they needed each other. Fed off each other. Ironbones had asked him once: "Without me, what are you?"

What was he, indeed? A shell, that's what. Messenger had stared into the abyss and the abyss had well and truly stared right back and got in his head.

And he did wonder what would become of him without Ironbones.

But the future could wait.

Now he had a job to do.

He strode up the slope.

IRONBONES

The mine shaft was lit only by a single bulb hanging from the damp, rocky ceiling. It dangled from a cable, like a hanged man swaying from the scaffold.

Messenger went down the passageway. His belly churned. This was it. He had trapped Ironbones. Tricked him and caged him.

And now he was going to kill him.

End this fucking thing once and for all. End it in the way it had begun. Using the forces that had created Ironbones to destroy him.

"Get it done," the police commissioner had said during a meeting, shuffling papers, not looking Messenger in the eye.

Messenger had looked around the room.

The commissioner; the assistant commissioner in charge of Met Ops, one of the four business group that form the Metropolitan Police Service; the home secretary and some of her senior civil servants; representatives of M15 and the military.

Too many bloody bosses, Messenger had thought at the time.

None of them looked at him. He was a damaged ex-cop. He was poison. Look at him, they'd been infected.

He was more or less a hired killer, now. They were sending him out to face the monster. Not supplying any rules of engagement. No guidelines, no directions, no responsibility.

Get it done.

A civil servant said, "Alive or dead."

Messenger had smiled before looking at every dignitary in the room. Still they didn't make eye contact.

Loud and clear, he had thought.

And dead or alive meant dead.

End it.

And that's what he would do.

He stepped out of the passageway and into the cavern. It was immense, a grim, rocky womb. A sort of cold, dark hell where a monster could be born. And where it would die.

And there was the monster in question—the devil himself.

"You can't kill me, Messenger," roared Ironbones, rattling the cage.

The enclosure hung from the ceiling on four chains.

Cage and chains were made of titanium—the strongest metal on earth to hold the strongest killer.

The metal had been used to build a submersible that withstood the pressure of deep-sea diving in the Mariana Trench, the deepest oceanic trench on earth. Titanium was used in planes, ships, spacecraft and missiles. It was heat resistant, wouldn't corrode, so was used to store nuclear waste.

And now it was being used to hold Ironbones.

Messenger walked up to the cage, looked up at it. The monster was a massive silhouette behind the bars. Messenger knew what that silhouette looked like. He had looked into its eyes many times. He'd faced it and had the scars to prove it. Ironbones's sickle—his weapon of choice—had sliced Messenger's flesh, often nearly killing him.

The attack on his home three years previously, which left his eldest child gutted, had seen Messenger hospitalized for six months with severe injuries.

What doesn't kill you makes you angrier.

Hands the size of spades reached through the bars. The pale flesh was covered in ritualistic tattoos.

"What makes you think you can kill me this time, Messenger?"

Its voice was quieter now, deep and guttural.

"You've never managed it before."

Messenger said nothing. He strode over to the wall where there was a large flip-handle switch. He gripped it and looked up at the cage.

Ironbones lunged forward, his terrifying face caught the cave's natural light.

"I will not die, Messenger," he snarled. "I am forever because someone loves me."

Messenger pulled the switch halfway down.

Blinding light filled the cave. Sparks flew in the cage. A roar shook the very mountain. Thousands and thousands of volts of electricity surged through cables, down the chains into the titanium cage.

Ironbones shrieked and was lit up like a firework.

He gripped the bars and rattled the cage violently, and his hands started to smoke and blacken.

He snarled at Messenger. Those sharpened teeth, which had torn human flesh so often, bared.

"I'll be back for you," he hissed.

"Not this time," Messenger said. "The dead should stay dead."

He pulled the lever all the way down. As sparks flew, Ironbones screamed, "Only the unloved—"

"Is it true that he dies, Miss Payne?"

Jane Cooper couldn't help herself. She had to know. Her sweaty hand gripped the novel: Ironbones: The Last Dance by Kaz Payne.

She had been first in line at Waterstones, had been outside the bookstore at 6:00 pm to make sure she was first.

It hadn't taken long for a queue to start forming behind her. Everyone wanted a copy of the book. But Jane was first.

She was the number one fan. She was the true believer. Knew every single line of every single Ironbones book.

Jane didn't move from her spot at the front of the queue. She even peed herself. The so-called fans behind her turned up their noses; shifted back a bit.

They shouted at her, called her a fat pig, said she was disgusting.

But she didn't care. She'd been shouted at and mocked all her life. She was waiting to get her hands on the final chapter in the story of the love of her life.

And the rumour was that Kaz Payne would be killing him off—for real this time.

Ironbones would die in the last book. There would not be another resurrection, apparently.

"Who shall I make it out to?" asked Kaz Payne, a small, neat woman with short, boyish blonde hair

Jane felt confused. "You don't remember?"

"Remind me."

"Jane, I'm Jane," said Jane, stating the obvious.

"Jane," said Kaz Payne, started to sign the book.

"You've signed all my books. I come to all your events. I know everything."

Kaz Payne finished signing, shut the book, handed it back. "Do you?"

“Are you in love with Gabriel Messenger?”

The author glanced over at someone, then, “I used to be.”

“Are you in love with Ironbones?”

The author paused and stared deep into Jane’s eyes. “He’s my child.”

“Then you’ve murdered your own child if you’ve killed him.”

Jane was quickly moved along by some scrawny kid who said, “Lots of people waiting.”

At the door, Jane hesitated. Glanced over her shoulder at Kaz Payne, who had everything, signing another copy for a so-called fan.

Then, Jane, who’d had her everything taken away from her if the rumours were true, turned and left the shop.

The rumours were true. At 4:15 am, she finished the book.

Jane was covered in sweat, her heart pounded. She stared at the last two words, the very last THE END apparently. All the other books had finished with the words TO BE CONTINUED.

Not this one. This was it. It was over.

Jane felt empty. A rage grew in her breast. Rage the likes of which you would not believe, she thought, recalling a quote from Frankenstein.

The smell of cat piss assailed her senses and her eyes watered. The music from upstairs thumped.

It was like coming back to the real world.

The dream was over. The fantasy she'd lived for a decade. Now it was truly back to the drudgery. Back to the bullying. Back to the isolation.

That had always happened after she'd finished reading an Ironbones book, of course. But previously she'd known there'd be another one in a year or so.

But not this time.

Jane had lived in this bedsit for thirteen years, lonely and loveless. Kaz Payne's Ironbones books had been her life raft. They'd helped her navigate the world, which for people like her—outsiders, weird, shy—was Hell.

And now the life raft was gone. No salvation. Nothing to look forward to. Kaz Payne had destroyed that—killed Jane's one true love. And, yes, just like Mary Shelly wrote, when love died, rage arose.

Jane looked around her flat and the reality of her life crashed into her. She blubbered uncontrollably. Snot and tears streamed down her face, all over her clothes.

She stared at the book. She looked at it as a mother would look upon her dying child as the infant took its final breath.

She would never see that child again.

Jane would never be in the company of Ironbones or Gabriel Messenger, his nemesis, again.

Sure, she could re-read the books; she often did. And she got a thrill from doing that. But it wasn't like the first time, was it. The first time was the special time.

Jane leapt off the couch. The cats scattered. The music thumped through the ceiling.

Fury was blinding her. She would always ignore the thudding thrash metal, which was often played through the night. It probably wouldn't matter if she had complained. Knocking on the door and asking them to please turn it down would only result in a "cunt" storm

"Fuck off, you cunt..."

"You fat, ugly cunt..."

"Get your cunt face away from my door..."

But now she was angry.

She strode into the kitchenette. Thrust her hand into the pile of dirty dishes in the sink. Yanked a bread knife out of the soiled, tepid water.

With her body tight, as if something else was in control of it, she stomped out of her flat.

Breathing heavily, she raced upstairs, the steps bucking beneath her two-hundred-and-fifty-pound frame.

Up on the second floor, the music was overwhelming; deafening. She found it hard to breathe. It was like being crushed by noise. The corridor shook to the roaring chords, the clashing cymbals, the pounding bass, the screeching voice.

She gritted her teeth. Her blood boiled. Hate made her shake—hate for the world, for Kaz Payne, for whoever lived in this flat.

She hammered on the door. Her temperature rose as she waited. After a few seconds, the door opened sharply.

The music exploded out of the flat, almost knocking Jane off her feet. The smell of dope swam out into the corridor.

The guy who'd opened the door was tall, pale-faced, bare-chested, lathered in tattoos.

"What, you fat fucking bitch?" he snarled in her face, showing missing teeth.

Every sinew and nerve in Jane's body was tight and she shook with wrath

She unleashed it with a shriek, lunged with the knife.

It was amazing to see the blade sink into his body, the stainless-steel sliding into skin, plunging deeply into the guy's chest.

His mouth gaped. His eyes shot open. He gurgled and stared down at the knife. There was a moment of stillness when they both gazed into each other's eyes. And Jane felt briefly that she could have loved him.

But then he croaked and staggered back into his flat.

The music was like a tornado.

Jane followed him into the apartment.

She slammed the door shut behind her.

He flailed, making a horrible noise; keening like a dying animal. Blood seeped from where the knife protruded.

He let out a weird hissing noise.

Jane gawped at him.

What had she done?

"Help me," he rasped.

He collapsed, taking his music with him. The entire system crashed to the floor. The music died. Jane stood in silence, watching her victim's death throes.

He was arching his back, clawing at his chest, fighting for breath.

Then, his eyes rolled back. His mouth opened wide. A farting noise came out of him. And he slumped. Dead.

Jane stared at the body.

And she had an orgasm.

Sex and death, and all that.

Karen Davies smoked outside the bookstore. It was 4:30 am. It had been a long night and the first hint of dawn appeared in the sky.

Workmen traipsed in and out of the shop, ferrying backdrops supplied by the publisher, Martells, into a van.

The backdrops depicted the cover of Ironbones: The Last Dance by Kaz Payne.

Karen liked being Kaz Payne. She'd been Kaz Payne for more than a decade now. And being Kaz Payne was certainly better than being some of the freaky fans who'd been practically stalking her all this time, obsessed by Ironbones.

She thought now of a particular fan. The one who'd earlier accused her of murdering her child.

That woman was a pathetic figure. Terrible clothes. Rings under her eyes. No make-up. Hair stringy. Dark stains on her smock. So overweight. And she smelled odd too; like piss.

"All done," a voice said.

She turned, stared right into John Drake's face.

"Happy now?" she asked bitterly.

He reached out to put his hands on her shoulders, but she jerked away.

"You lost the right to touch me a long time ago," she said.

He held out his hands as if in surrender. They stood in silence. Watched the workmen going about their business.

Eventually Drake said, "It's for the best."

"It is for you."

"For us, Karen. You can forget about this Ironbones stuff, forget about this curse. Concentrate on decent stuff."

"Decent stuff? What do you know about decency?"

He snatched the cigarette out of her hand and puffed on it before dropping it and crushing it under foot.

He shook with rage. "Can't believe you wrote another one. You still haven't done what I told you, what I advised as your manager—delete the fucking thing."

She said nothing.

"This was the end, Karen. That's what you said."

"He's in me, can't let go that easily."

He glared at her. Something on the tip of his tongue. He kept it there, blew it out in a puff of air, and said, "Lay this ghost to rest. Focus of what you've been contracted to write. Think of all the bloody contract, Karen. You can be a great writer, you know."

"I am a great writer. But then—you weren't a great detective were you."

"Don't make a scene."

"That's what I do, John darling—make scenes. So real and so bloody that you and your boys in blue could do nothing about it."

"That's enough."

She got another cigarette out of the packet, lit it, said, "One of the fans told me I'd murdered him."

"Nutters."

"They have insight."

"Into what? Their own empty lives?"

"Into his soul."

"Who's fucking soul, Karen?"

"You know."

"He's made up. Jesus, I sometimes wonder if you're not as nuts as some of your readers."

"Maybe I am."

"Can I take you home?"

"No you fucking can't. Don't try it on just because you think I'm vulnerable. I'm not."

"Didn't suggest—"

"Someone else will die, you know that."

He stared at her. "You know this, do you?"

"Yes, and so do you. Someone always dies."

Jane wondered how long it would take for a dead body to start smelling.

She glanced up at the ceiling as she entered her bedsit, thinking about the body upstairs.

She had dug around the flat upstairs while its tenant lay dead and found that he was called Aaron James. There were some bills addressed to him. If he was Aaron James, of course. He could be someone else; someone just crashing there. Or a new tenant. Aaron James might have moved on and forgotten to fill in a change-of-address form at the Post Office.

Ultimately, it didn't matter. She had also scoured the dingy man-cave for anything she could salvage. There were some tins of food in the cupboard, which she tossed into a plastic bag she found under the sink.

After cramming her haul into her own cupboards, she went back upstairs with a bottle of bleach and threw it over everything: the body, the smashed-up stereo, the carpet, the CDs. She emptied the bottle and the place smelled brutally clean.

She had no idea if it would work, of course, if her efforts would destroy any forensics. But she might as well give it a go.

Then she went downstairs, exhausted.

It was nearly 6:00 am.

She snuggled up on the couch, where she always slept. Tucked herself under the blankets. Fell asleep. Dreamed of walking hand in hand with Ironbones. Above them a red sky. Beneath their feet a scorched earth. Surrounding them on both sides, dunes of dead bodies: rotting, mutilated.

She woke up sweating two hours later.

First thing she did was to put the copy of Ironbones: The Last Dance on the shelf with the others in the collection.

She usually bought the hardback edition when it came out. A few months later the paperback edition would be published, and she'd buy that too—and read it.

She'd also download the Kindle ebook edition and get her hands on as many foreign-language editions as she could. Editions in French, German, Portuguese, Italian, Mandarin, Japanese, Czech, Danish—and so many other languages—crammed her special Ironbones bookshelf.

She also had paraphernalia—mugs, figurines, posters.

There was also a full-sized cut-out of the psycho himself in the corner of her bedsit.

He looked amazingly menacing and gorgeous to Jane.

He was seven-feet two-inches of bulging muscles and tattoos. Bald head, filed teeth, a missing ear lost in the first book when a policeman called Allport sliced it off with an axe.

Ironbones had laughed in the face of adversity, picked up the ear—and eaten it.

Eaten his own ear. Then ruined Allport. Sawed him in half.

Jane remembered reading that, nearly ten years ago now, and feeling shocked and excited that someone cared so little.

But Ironbones's death at the hands of—Jane couldn't even think about it, now, without welling up.

How could they have done that? How could a mother...? No feelings. No love.

But that was Jane's problem—she loved too much. She wanted not to love. She wanted to be a machine like Ironbones. Just do whatever she wanted to do without a care in the world. He was only driven by his desire, and that desire was to cause catastrophe.

Jane didn't necessarily want to cause catastrophe, but she wished she had Ironbones's will.

She stared at the cut-out. She felt something funny inside her. She wanted to masturbate. Ironbones couldn't die. Kaz Payne wouldn't be allowed to kill him; no way.

Jane spooned some food into the cats' bowls. Thought about clearing out the litter trays but didn't bother. Scuttled out of the flat again.

Karen seethed.

Drake was on TV saying: "Kaz Payne has decided to end this series of novels, primarily because she has other stories to tell."

She was sitting at the desk in the dim-lit hotel room where many of the Ironbones books had been written, where he'd been created.

She was watching the interview surrounded by posters of her creation: a large cut-out, over seven-feet tall; Ironbones mugs, T-shirts, lampshades; bookshelves loaded with different versions of her books—hardback, paperback, translations, graphic-novel editions.

There was even a kids edition, for Christ's sake. But that was a rare copy as most of those were pulped.

There had been a furore when it was published. Karen, at the time, thought it was a terrible idea. But the publisher was all for it.

Press went ballistic, of course. Copies were burned, and not for the first time. Karen lapped it up—good publicity for the actual adult versions of her books.

Now it was over, however. Or the likes of Drake were trying to tell her it was over.

Karen's fury grew. She grabbed an Ironbones mug, crushed it. Her knuckles grew white. Drake had recorded the interview that morning. She cursed herself for not demanding to know what he was going to say. But she was tired, under pressure.

Drake rambled on.

"Kaz is an extremely talented writer. She is now working on a new novel. We have a deal with a major publisher, as everyone knows. The novel will feature a feisty female private investigator."

The interviewer said, "That's very exciting, John. Of course, as her former boyfriend, and still her manager, you have a unique perspective on her work, her life. How has this Ironbones series affected her?"

Drake pondered. Karen fumed.

He said, "First, let me stress that although we are no longer a couple, we're good friends. However, to have been labelled a cheap, pulp writer hurt her a lot."

Karen hurled the mug at the TV. China shattered as it hit the floor. The screen buckled and went black.

Now the room was virtually in darkness.

Just how she liked it.

Only the sliver of moonlight sneaking in through the partially closed curtains made it possible to see anything.

Karen made her way to a bookshelf. She ran her finger across the spines, came to the one she was looking for. Slid the book out.

Switching on the torch on her iPhone, she illuminated the cover of the book.

Ironbones: The First Cut.

The one that started it all. More than a decade ago.

She opened the book to Chapter One, started reading:

Ironbones was born in a furnace of fury and chaos and hatred. A storm raged. Lightning tore at the fabric of the sky, its violent, bright forks providing a brief glimpse to the terrible world beyond this one. Crone lay in pools of her own fluid, and roared with—

There was a knock at the door.

Karen flinched. She slammed the book shut, placed it on her desk. Thought: Who the fuck is that at this time? And who knew about this place?

Suspiciously, she went to the door.

Drake was partying with her publishers, so it wouldn't be him. She'd made her excuses. Had no interest attending what she regarded as a wake.

Whoever was there knocked again.

She switched on the light. The bulb flickered. She hesitated. Taking out her phone, she tapped an app that allowed her to see who was outside her door. On the camera, she saw a short, pudgy figure wearing a hood.

Karen spoke into the microphone on the phone.

"What do you want?"

The visitor, suddenly hearing a voice above their head, looked up and stared directly at the camera.

Karen recognized her straight away.

The fan.

"What is it?" Karen said. "It's nearly 10:00 pm."

The woman said, "You can't kill him."

Karen hesitated. She thought about something before going to open the door.

Someone has to die, she thought. Someone has always died.

Jane couldn't believe it. She was in Kaz Payne's sanctuary. The place where she created Ironbones. A secret place not many people had access too. A squalid little hovel in a grubby little hotel.

Jane was thinking about her own squalid little hovel. There was hope, then. But you had to have talent; she had none.

Still, the next best thing to being an angel was to be among them. This was like being in the holy of holies in the Temple in Jerusalem, right next to the place where God lived.

Rumour was that Kaz Payne had bough the hotel so she could use this room to write. Lots of dark corners here. Places were evil could lurk. It was exciting. All the memorabilia, the books. So similar to Jane's flat. She and Kaz clearly had a lot in common.

She looked over at the cut-out of Ironbones. She felt a little thrill because she had one just like it, and she said, "I have one just like it."

The author looked taken aback. "Do you? Where did you get it?"

"On eBay."

"Of course. Tell me, how did you know where to find me?"

"I'm your number one fan."

"Obviously."

Jane looked around the gloomy little room. It was tiny and a bit grotty. Papers piled everywhere. Manuscripts crammed onto shelves. Stuff she herself owned: mugs, posters, figurines. And the books, of course—lots of them.

She pointed at the manuscripts and asked, "Are they the originals?"

"Some of them are, yes. Various drafts."

Something raced through Jane's blood. They must be worth a fortune. But she would never sell them if she owned them. They would be too precious. It would be like finding the original copies of the Gospels. You would just keep them, maybe copy them. But not sell them for a quick buck.

Jane would rather sell her own soul than take something as valuable as that to an auction and allow philistines to get their grubby hands on them.

"Why don't you want him to die?" the author asked out of the blue.

Jane's mouth fell open, and she looked at Payne, who was sitting behind her desk, gently rocking back and forth on her swivel chair.

Jane had a cold sweat. It was just like those therapists she'd always had to see. Talking about her fears, about her father and the things he did to her and how, despite all those things, she still craved his love.

She shook her head.

"You all right?" the author asked.

"Yes, sorry."

"Do you want to meet him?"

"What?"

"Ironbones."

"Meet him?" Jane couldn't grasp what the author was saying. She sensed something move in the shadows behind Payne. Jane flinched. Nothing there. Moonlight shifting as the curtain wafted, that's all; shadows.

Payne said, "You're a super-fan, aren't you?"

"I am, I really am."

Something passed across the author's face: fear, maybe. But then it was gone. She said, "I guess since it's the end—"

"So it is the end?" She'd read the book but came here looking for hope.

"Since it's—what was your name?"

"Jane."

"Since it's the end, Jane, and you're, well, you're the number one fan, you should have this great honour bestowed upon you."

"W-what great honour?"

Something huge shifted in the gloom behind Kaz Payne.

Jane's eyes widened to take in the darkness.

KISSING THE ENVELOPE

12 years earlier...

"NO, KAREN, I'LL do it," Connie Wishaw said.

"I want to."

Karen held up the ten-pound note, trying to attract the barman's attention. But he was busy. Friday nights at the Feathers—a traditional pub-turned-trendy-wine bar—were full-on. Hundreds of young people awash with cash, flashing it at the bar staff.

Karen Davies was not one of them.

Twenty-three, she was skint. But she needed this drink. She needed to be out on the town with her best mate Connie. She needed to buy her best mate Connie a drink.

"You can't be buying rounds all night," Karen said, slightly worse for wear after the girls had shared two bottles of wine at their flat in Hoxton before they headed into town; the West End.

Connie worked in the City, a young broker with an investment bank.

She and Karen had been schoolfriends in Kent. Lost touch when both went to university. Reconnected just a year ago over Facebook. Discovered they lived a few miles apart in the capital.

Connie with a plan, Karen with a dream.

The dream of being a chick lit author.

From the age of fourteen, when she completed her first novel, Karen had been determined to be the next Jennifer Weiner—not only an author but a commentator. Someone the media approached for their opinions. She wanted to be "it", or an it-girl.

But things were not going well.

Apart from the good fortune to reacquaint with Connie, life was rotten.

Karen was on her backside.

About to be kicked out her of flat, she'd mournfully trawled Facebook, basically looking for old friends. Nostalgia really comes at you hard in times of trouble. You crave your old life. The one you see through rose-tinted glasses.

Fortuitously, she linked up with Connie on the social-media site. And they arranged to meet up.

"So how are things with you?" Connie has asked after regaling Karen with her success.

Karen had burst into tears. Connie had said, "Come live with me, there's a spare room."

"I could never afford the rent."

"It's in Hoxton, up and coming, nothing flash. And my dad bought it for me. I'll charge you a cheap-as-chips rent."

It was cheap-as-chips, too. Karen moved in. Continued working late shifts at Tesco. Wrote during the day.

Wrote a lot.

Completed novels in two months. She once finished one in a week, fuelled by Red Bull and Pro Plus. Not a good combo.

But if you wanted success, you had to sacrifice. Although it did puzzle Karen as to how much exactly you needed to sacrifice before the gods were satisfied and gave you salvation.

Karen's luck never turned. She received rejection after rejection, especially from George Ellis at Parlour Publishing, a group dedicated to women's fiction of all kinds, from Mills & Boon-type slush to what was referred to as "female-led erotica".

Between going off to university in Manchester at the age of eighteen to study English—which resulted in a paltry third—and right now at the Feathers in the West End, Karen had sent twelve completed novels to Parlour.

Each had been rejected. And with each rejection, Ellis's impatience grew. Initially he and his firm were charitable and supportive.

"Keep writing..."

"Good luck with your efforts..."

"It's a difficult industry..."

and so on; but as the submissions increased, the rejections became less tolerant of her ambition:

"Perhaps another genre..."

"Very much the same as we've read before..."

"Lacking some structure..."

And much worse, too.

"Don't give up," Connie had said, before adding, "Dad needs that two-hundred quid rent."

And then came the latest rejection:

"We are beginning to wonder if publishing might not be your thing, Miss Davies," the letter said after Karen had sent Slack Alice, a "chick-lit comedy about a lazy girl who finds a reason to get busy".

"At least you get letters," Connie had said. "Don't a lot of authors get nothing at all?"

That was true. But Karen sometimes thought the void of nothingness would be preferable.

The barman came up to her, smiled.

Karen fluttered her eyelashes said: "Two vodka and Red Bull."

"Want ice?"

"Please."

He prepped the drinks, brought them over, took her tenner.

She turned to hand one drink to Connie, but her friend wasn't there. Karen spotted her straight away. At a table chatting to two guys.

Karen sighed. Here we go.

The guy groaned and came.

Karen sighed. Didn't come. Clawed his back.

He rolled off her and she looked at the ceiling.

Here it comes, she thought.

"Nice, babe," said the guy.

He was late twenties. Nice looking. Tall and lean. No body hair apart from his pubic area. He worked in IT for a leading bank.

The guy got out of bed and Karen took a moment to stare at his ass. It was tight and tanned. With his back to her, the guy took off his condom. He did something with it; wrapped it in a tissue or a cloth or something. Put on his boxers and said, “Bathroom?”

“Down the corridor, second on the left.”

The guy went to sort himself out.

Karen flexed her hips, got out of bed naked and sat at her desk.

She opened up her laptop, turned it on.

She double clicked the Word file on her desktop, a novel she was writing called Heart’s Quest.

Nothing happened.

She waited. Sweat ran down the back of her neck. Fluid ran down the inside of her leg.

She swallowed, double clicked again.

Nothing happened again.

She felt dizzy; her belly churned.

Fuck, she thought.

Again she tried to open the file, but once more nothing happened.

Rage boiled in her blood... I have love in me... she bunched her fists... the likes of which... she started to punch her own arm in fury, gasping... you can scarcely imagine... head spinning, feeling sick, voice in her head...

She gave a shout of anger after trying to open the file for a fourth time.

Then she started to click frenziedly on the icon.

"Open, you cunt," she screamed.

"What's the problem, babe?"

She wheeled round.

The guy's eyes went down to her tits. They must've shaken when she spun around in her chair. He gave a little smile. He was in his Calvin Klein's and looked good. She stared at his package, spoke to it.

"File," she said. "Nothing happening."

She could barely speak. She was a bonfire of wrath. Hell played out in her head. Fiery lakes, vicious demons, suffering souls.

"Let me have a look," the package said.

Karen got out of her seat. The guy looked her up and down. Took her chair. He crunched his knuckles.

Karen pulled on the ragged old Nirvana T-shirt she usually wore to bed.

The guy called up a file on her laptop—just lines and lines of computer language.

Karen swallowed. Her mouth was dry. The walls felt as if they were closing in. A voice in her head was calling her name. A male voice: deep, guttural. She ignored it. Had no clue what it was. It was weirdly clear; as if something lived in her skull. Perhaps she should go back to see her therapist again. She'd had to see one for anger issues when she was a teenager.

"Heart's Quest, yeah?" the guy asked.

Karen said, "Yeah," and stood behind him.

The file opened.

"Easy," the guy said. "It was just your..."

A jumble of technical words that Karen didn't understand poured from his cute mouth. Like every practical man, this guy really wanted to go through the ins and outs just to show off. Karen let him ramble on. Stared at the screen. The words she'd written were salvaged.

She finally said, "Thanks. Can I sit down now?"

But he was reading. "Jesus, did you write this?"

She grabbed the back of the chair, crushed it. "Can I sit down?"

"This is slushy," he said.

Karen shook the chair and shouted: "Can I fucking sit down."

The guy gawped at her, got up. "Sorry, babe."

She was ruffled, wanting him to leave.

"Thanks," she said. "Really, thanks."

That's okay."

She thought for a moment. Perhaps "thanks" wasn't enough. Half-heartedly she asked: "Shall we see each other again?"

He smiled. "Nah."

She wrote the rest of the night.

The novel had to be finished because she wanted to send it to Parlour first thing as it was a Thursday.

It would mean the package would arrive at the publisher on Friday. Just in time for the weekend when many manuscripts were read.

It was the third draft of Heart's Quest, a new venture for Karen—a Regency romance.

Set in the early 19th century, it told the story of Georgina Heart, a "pretty and independent heiress whose family had fallen on hard times when her father ran off to America with his mistress—and the family fortune". Georgina sails to the United States in pursuit of her father. In the U.S., she naturally finds love with a "ruggedly handsome pioneer homesteader" named Cutler Forrest.

Karen hoped the novel would be the first in a series. It was her best work. She'd sweated blood over it, barely sleeping. She would go to work at Tesco at midnight to stack shelves, finish at 6:00 am. By 7:00 am she'd be back home, and worked solidly for three hours, fuelled by Red Bull and Pro Plus.

At 10:00 am she would collapse on her bed. Sleep for five hours before getting up and eating soup or something on toast. By about 4:00 pm, she was back at the computer working on her novel. She'd nap again between 8:00 pm and 11:00pm, before getting ready for her Tesco shift. Back on the treadmill. Same thing, day after day.

Even on her two-days-off a week, she barely stopped; kept writing. Connie had to drag her out of the house sometimes.

Working now, she thought it was a good thing Connie had persuaded her to go out last night.

She wouldn't have met what's-his-name who fixed her laptop, saved her story.

By now she would have probably killed someone.

She checked her phone: 7:00 am.

Fatigue suddenly overwhelmed her. But she was nearly done. While the document printed, Karen pulled herself together. She showed it the baby wipes; sprayed some dry shampoo on her blonde hair.

By the time she was ready, the document had printed, and she neatly stacked all the pages before putting them into an envelope with a cover letter she had already written.

She went downstairs with the package, put it on the countertop, grabbed a coffee.

Connie was there, dressed to kill, swigging a green-coloured juice.

"Is that it?" she asked, noticing the package.

Karen nodded.

She came over and picked the package up; went to kiss it.

Karen snatched it out her hands.

Connie's face paled.

Karen said, "Maybe that's the problem."

"What? Me kissing the envelope?"

"You've always done it."

"To wish it luck."

"It's never worked."

"It's just a bit of fun, Kaz."

"Yeah, but maybe you curse it."

Connie pulled a face; a what the fuck are you talking about? face, and said, "Come on. You sent plenty of shit books out that got rejected way before I started kissing the envelope."

A blaze ignited in Karen's breast. She glared at Connie, who's face dropped; realized her fuck-up.

"Sorry, Kaz," she said. "Didn't mean that."

Karen said nothing. Grabbed the package and stormed out. She felt a hurting deep inside, a hate for the world that pulsed like a huge, dark-red sun.

And in her mind, her imagination, she scorched the entire earth.

Waiting was always the worst.

Most writers say you should start another project after submitting your manuscript. Karen guessed most writers didn't do this. Most writers were liars, she thought. Just said the right things. Never practised what they preached.

The truth was that everyone was broken. Everyone desperate for approval. And when approval didn't come, it left scars.

She lay in bed thinking. It was 3:00 pm. She'd done her Tesco stint. Got home just before 7:00 am, started typing gibberish into her laptop: ideas for the next novel.

She let out a cry of frustration, slammed the laptop shut. This was her last attempt, she decided. Heart's Quest was her own heart's quest. It was different to her earlier efforts, and she was really optimistic about it.

But she just couldn't keep putting herself out there; couldn't expose herself to more rejection, more hurt.

Connie always read Karen's manuscripts, and often just said, "Yeah, it's cool, babe."

But Connie didn't really read.

So Karen never believed her. She supplied only vague comments like yeah that's good, good plot, reads well, and so on.

Karen had no one else to read her books. Very few friends. Her work colleagues rarely read. No one read. Not even Karen.

Christ, you don't read, she thought to herself.

It was a shocking revelation.

She clutched her chest as if she was having a heart attack.

I want to be a writer and I don't read, she thought.

As if it were imperative, or she would die, she darted across the room to the bookshelf.

It was dusty, a cheap Ikea thing. The spines of the books shoved on the shelf were cracked and creased. As if they'd been read and read and read again.

Not by me, she thought.

She scanned the titles. She could hardly remember buying—or maybe stealing—any of them. Cheap paperbacks mostly.

She chose one, slid it out. Looked at the cover. Some cheap romance. But you had to start somewhere.

Karen lay on her bed and started to read, but she soon drifted off with the book open on her chest.

She'd woken with a start, checked her phone: 3:00 pm.

She tossed the book aside. Leapt off the bed. Scurried downstairs. Something came to mind. Something in her head. She was trying to recall whatever it was—a dream, a voice. But her mind was blurry. Never mind, she thought, and let it go.

In the hallway, there was a pile of post. She filed through it: bills, circulars, spam.

But then —

A letter addressed to her, stamped with Parlour Publishing's logo.

Her heart skipped a beat. She staggered into the kitchen. Sat at the table. Stared at the envelope.

Her mouth was dry. Her eyes cakey with sleep.

Wee, she thought. I need a wee.

She went to the toilet. Had a piss. Clawed her arms. Came back.

The letter as still there, spiting her. Mocking. Daring her to open it.

She knew what it would say.

They all said the same thing in so many words:

Fuck off.

Maybe this one would actually use those words, too: One last time, Miss Davies: FUCK OFF.

She grabbed handfuls of hair and gave out a frustrated roar.

Open it you coward, she thought.

She grabbed it. Stared at it. Tore it open. Scrunched up the envelope and threw it aside.

She put the letter down flat on the table and, mouth agape, read it.

"A meeting?" Connie said. "A fucking meeting?"

She was reading the letter. They were in the kitchen. Karen was tempted to open a bottle of wine. It was 7:00 pm, after all, Connie having just come back from work.

"That is what it says, isn't it?" Karen asked, thinking this might be a dream and she would soon wake up.

"It's what it says, Kaz."

"Read it for me."

"Again?"

Karen nodded.

Connie read: "Dear Karen, Thank you for sending us your latest novel. Your tenacity is to be admired. Perhaps we should finally meet and have a conversation about your work. Ring my secretary to arrange—signed, George Ellis, publisher."

"A meeting, that's what it says."

"Yes, Kaz."

"But what do you think he means, Con?"

Connie chuckled. "It means he wants a meeting."

"Not to discuss the novel though; not to discuss Heart's Quest."

"Seems obvious. It's a really good novel."

"Don't lie, you never read it."

Connie shrugged. "I might do now it's getting published."

Karen hesitated. Darkness descended. "You didn't think I'd ever get published, did you?"

Connie looked flustered, went red. "You what?"

Karen went to the fridge and took out a bottle of wine. Poured herself a glass without offering Connie one, said, "You told me I'd sent loads of shit books out. We were talking about you kissing the envelope for luck. Few weeks ago."

Connie's face went even redder. Licked her lips. "I don't remember. Sorry anyway." She flapped her hand, dismissing her comment if she'd ever made it, said, "Forget about what's happened in the past, all the rejections, just look to the future. Let's celebrate and—"

"I didn't let you kiss it, did I—not this time."

Connie shrugged. "It was just a bit of fun. Why are you even—"

Karen said, "Cow." She felt empty; a vacuum. "You never believed in me. Never had my back. Thought my writing was a waste of time."

"I offered you a home on the cheap, you cheeky sod."

"Maybe you liked having me around. Someone to pity. To look down at while you soared. Someone no good to compare yourself to."

"Kaz, what the fuck are you—"

"I'm really surprised you never told me to get a proper job."

"You-you've got one."

"You reckon my writing is a proper job?"

"No, the Tesco thing."

Karen felt as if she'd been hit—actually slapped hard across the face. She said, "When you mention me to your mates, if you ever bother, what do you say I do?"

"What do you mean?"

"Do you say I'm a writer?"

"Come on, Kaz, writing's not a job, is it."

Karen said nothing.

Connie poured herself a glass of wine. "You don't make money out of it, do you. A job is something you make a living out of."

"What if I did make a living out of it?"

Connie spluttered spitefully, bringing the glass to her mouth. "Come on, Kaz."

Karen had no clue where the rage came from, where it was born in her. But it was like a clear white light exploding silently in her head—a big-bang event, an expansion of pure hate throughout her entire being.

With the flat of her hand, she uppercut the base of the wine glass Connie had just brought up to her mouth. The rim shattered against Connie's lips and teeth and gums. The jagged part of the bowl severed her flesh. Serrated glass sliced into her tongue. Shards frayed her nostrils, turning them into strands of flesh.

Blood sprayed everywhere. Connie shrieked, her torn-up face creasing in agony.

She staggered back, dropping the broken glass, spilling wine. Blood poured from her mutilated face. She was screeching, flailing, crashing into things.

But Karen did nothing—just watched her friend bleed and scream. And sort of enjoyed it, too.

"My client pleads guilty, your Honour."

Her lawyer had said it was for the best—just get it over with. On top of the fact that she had blatantly done it.

Karen stood in the dock. It had been a serious enough assault for her case to be sent to Crown Court, and now she just glared at the judge.

After the attack, Connie had called the police and screamed at them through her torn-to-shreds mouth.

There was blood all over the place. The kitchen floor was soaked in it. Karen had stared, fascinated, as it poured from her friend's face.

She was arrested when the police arrived. As they were taking her out in handcuffs she said to Connie, "Just toss my stuff into the big sports bag you'll find under the bed."

Connie cried. Paramedics were looking after her. She stared at Karen with a new look—fear.

To Karen, this had been a distraction. She was desperate to meet up with George Ellis. After being charged and released on police bail, she had called the publisher's secretary and arranged a meeting. It was to be in a month, when this business with the assault would have been done and dusted.

Conditions attached to her bail included living at another address and not contacting Connie. Neither had been an issue for Karen. She didn't want to be near Connie now, had nothing to say to her.

Her so-called friend had shown her true colours. Connie didn't have her back when it came to her ambitions; she regarded them as a waste of time. So fuck her. And fuck her face too.

As to getting a place to live, she holed up in a down-and-out hotel in Earl's Court. It was grubby and seedy, smelled of piss and stale food. English was not the primary language of neither staff nor most of the guests. The other residents looked either to have been abused or abusers. Skinny, scared looking girls; heavy-set, hard-faced men.

She paid for a month upfront. Just had enough to cover that. Set up her laptop in the room. The only thing that mattered now was work. She had a meeting with George Ellis. He was going to offer her a deal. Things were looking up despite the prospect of prison.

"If you admit your guilt, show remorse, issue a heartfelt apology to Miss Wishaw, and as it is your first offence, you might avoid custody," her solicitor had said.

"'Might' is a word I probably would've preferred you'd left out of that sentence," Karen told her. "Replaced it with 'will', maybe."

The lawyer had sniffed. Something Connie found hard to do these days. But tough. She shouldn't have been a bitch.

Now the judge said, "Due the to the extreme nature of the attack on the victim—"

Shit, Karen thought. Her bones shook: here we go.

"— the offender would normally be looking at a period in custody."

OK; better, she thought.

"However—and it is a considerable however —"

Whatever.

"— due to the defendant's remorse, her quick guilty plea, and that it is her first offence —"

She got a hefty fine, probation and a community service order.

Connie and her family were appalled.

Thank goodness for British justice, thought Karen as she strode out of court.

A few days later, still holed up in her grubby hotel room, Karen got ready for her meeting at Parlour Publishing.

She hadn't slept the night before. All kinds of scenarios had been running through her mind. She couldn't switch them off. They kept replaying, over and over, and they did her head in.

She made herself a coffee using the sachets provided by the hotel. Turning the TV on, she picked up the aerial and moved it towards the window, searching for a signal. There was no cable here, no Wi-Fi. It was a 21st century Victorian slum; a shithole

She was killing time now. Checking her watch. Gazing blankly at the breakfast news. Swigging her coffee without thinking what she was doing.

Then something on TV caught her eye. She dropped the coffee cup. It hit the ground, spilling hot black liquid all over the already-stained with god-knows-what carpet.

Connie was on TV. Her face was make-up free. Scars laced her mouth, her jaw. Her lips were swollen. Teeth missing too. And her nose looked a mess—like someone had cut it with scissors and tried to glue it back together, but badly.

She wore a dark suit, her hair pulled back. She'd certainly gone for non-sexy, which was unusual for Connie.

"Recently," the presenter said, grim-faced, "Connie Wishaw sat in court watching a woman who glassed her violently —"

What other way is there to glass someone? Karen thought.

" — escape jail —"

I didn't escape jail, Karen thought, I avoided jail

" — while Connie herself has a life sentence, her pretty face now mutilated beyond repair."

You have no idea what mutilated actually looks like, Karen thought.

The presenter turned to Connie and said, "Tell us how Karen Davies's sentence made you feel?"

"It made me feel like I was the one being sentenced," Connie said. "She attacked me for no reason at all. Unprovoked. We were friends. Very good friends. I gave her a roof over her head when she was homeless —"

Fucking cow, Karen thought, grinding her teeth, clawing her arm.

" — on her knees, without a penny to her name. We'd been friends since school. I was lucky enough to have a decent job in the City. But Karen had struggled. Found life hard. So I decided to help her, be a good friend. And this is how she repaid me." Connie cried on cue.

The presenter asked, "Do you think the sentences handed out for this kind of attack, an attack that maims the victim for life, should be harsher?"

Pulling herself together, Connie said, "I absolutely do. There should be a crime of maiming with intent on the statue book. Because that's what Karen Davies did to me. She maimed me with intent. Acid attacks carry long jail sentence.

Glassing should be in the same category. I suffered life-changing injuries. I'll never be pretty again."

Connie burst into tears once more. The presenter reached across to comfort her.

Karen drew a blood-red streak with her lipstick across the TV screen.

Connie's weeping face was smeared scarlet.

George Ellis was a bloated buffoon in his early fifties, wearing a pink jacket with a red carnation in the buttonhole. His hair was oiled back on his scalp, and he had a tiny white scar on his tanned right cheek.

I'll show you scars, Karen thought.

But not now. Now she had to smile. Now she had to put on a happy face. She was, after all, the author of Heart's Quest.

Ellis had the manuscript in front of him on the desk. He was about to offer her a deal, finally. So she had to behave.

"Do you like my offices?" he asked.

Karen took a quick glance. It was a traditional room. Osborne & Little wallpaper. Antique furniture. Posters of Parlour front covers. A view of St John's Wood through the window.

"Parlour was established by my grandfather," Ellis said. "We have a reputation of being somewhat traditionalist, but you know, Miss Davies, we have diversified over the years and publish all kinds of romantic subsets"—he raised his eyebrows—"even erotica."

Karen was on tenterhooks, said nothing.

"How long have you been writing?" he asked.

Her mouth was dry. He hadn't offered her a drink of any sort. No water even. That set her nerves jangling. Should she read anything into it? Too late, she already had.

"All my life, writing little stories. I decided to be a writer when I was fourteen. It became an obsession."

"Indeed it did," Ellis said, eyebrows arching again.

Karen knitted her brow.

Ellis continued. "And what makes you think you are, or could be, an author, Miss Davies?"

Her mouth opened to answer but nothing came out. She looked around, seeking a response from the universe—the powers that were unseen. It was an odd question for him to ask. She looked at Ellis, thought for a second, then,

"What makes me think that is that I have the desire, the discipline, and the..." She tailed off. Was about to say "talent" then thought better of it. Went on after a moment. "It's the only thing I think about. And I work really hard at it. I've sacrificed so much. And I've written so much, too—been productive. And that's important. Shows I wouldn't be a one-hit wonder."

Ellis guffawed and said, "You're certainly productive. You've sent most of your productivity to me over the years."

"And you've rejected all of it—every book I sent you."

"For good reason, Miss Davies—they just weren't good enough."

He'd said "weren't", past tense. So did that mean Heart's Quest was good enough. Her belly flip-flopped.

"Please, I really want to be published."

He hesitated, left a gap into which Karen tossed all her hopes. Then he said, "We don't always get what we want."

Something buckled in Karen—the girders that hold your sanity in place, maybe.

"How old are you, Miss Davies?"

"Just turned twenty-four."

"Young, still young," he said.

"What does that mean?"

"Many authors don't make it until later in life, you know."

Her head filled with static. It was weird. As if someone had installed a radio in her skull. Turned it on. Was trying to tune it in. A voice seemed to be buried in the white noise. She couldn't make it out, but it sounded like someone calling out to her.

Ellis went on. "That's the kindest thing I can tell you. That maybe you are too young. Not yet fully-developed as an author."

A fissure cracked open in her belly and jetted steam right up into her head. Her face was hot and sweaty, her nape prickled.

"I've written fifty novels," she said, rasping. "I think that's developed, wouldn't you say?"

Ellis sighed. "But none of them have been published, Miss Davies. They've all be rejected. You, right now, are being rejected, my dear. You're not good enough."

She gripped the arms of the chair and squeezed.

The static in her head hissed. The voice in the white noise became clearer.

Unleash love, unleash me, it seemed to say. Vent it, vent your love.

"But this is what I've always wanted," she said, her voice breaking.

"What we always want is not what we always get. You're persistent, I'll give you that. But I won't give you the pleasure of seeing your novels in print. Not this one, not any you've sent me. I've written you rejection after rejection. But each time you bounce back up and send me more banality."

"Banality?" she said, tears welling.

"It's time to be cruel to be kind."

"You're being cruel to be cruel."

"Miss Davies, I invited you here to say this: Stop sending me your manuscripts. Stop thinking you'll ever be a writer. Stop writing."

Tears poured down Karen's face.

Ellis wasn't very sympathetic. Seen this nonsense, these tears, many times before. "Oh, do stop crying, this is not the end of the world, you know. I've not told you you're dying."

"You have, you bastard. You've killed me."

He rolled his eyes. "Go away, Miss Davies. Get a decent job. A nice career. You're a clever enough girl. Perhaps you'll find some work in the City like that friend of yours you mutilated."

Karen felt as if her body had turned to concrete. She was so rigid she couldn't move.

The voice in the static growled in her head:

Let me be your rage, butcher him for you.

She leapt to her feet. Grabbed her chair. Picked it up. Hurled it directly at Ellis, whose eyes widened with fear, and he moved far quicker than his portly frame suggested he could've done under normal circumstances.

He threw himself down. Gave a little squeal as he hit the floor. The chair smashed the oak-panelled wall behind him, taking chunks out of the wood.

Ellis lay on the varnished floor, red-faced and flustered, every hair out of place.

"Get out of my office, you crazy bitch."

Karen stormed out, roughly shouldering past Ellis's secretary who was coming into the office at the time to see what all the commotion was about.

Banality.

What a brutal word. I'll show you banality, she thought as she tore her hotel room to pieces.

The TV, already smeared in lipstick, was now on the floor, the screen cracked.

She was ripping the wallpaper down with her bare hands.

She lost nails doing it. Left streaks of blood on the thin wall that separated her room from the one next door.

But she was oblivious to pain. All she knew was rage. And that static in her head, the voice coming out of it, urged her on.

"Love is rage, rage is love! Unleash your love, unleash your rage!"

She didn't analyse it. Never once thought where it was coming from or why it was so enticing. She just went on the rampage.

She wheeled round, looking for something else to destroy.

Her laptop sat on the bed.

She froze, stared at it.

"Kill it," said the voice.

She lunged at the computer like a cat at a mouse. Picked it up and gave a cry of rage as she was about to fling it against the wall. Something caught her tear-filled eyes: moonlight catching steel. Just a moment, that was all, a flicker of an image.

She stopped dead.

What was it? It looked like a sickle—a nasty looking one. With a serrated blade. The image had only been in her mind's eye for less than a second, but it was clear to her.

She slumped on the bed, exhausted.

It's over, she thought. Everything is finished. I've wasted my life.

There was a knock at the door.

She didn't move.

Another knock and a voice, the Egyptian man at the reception desk, saying, "Everything all right in there?"

"Everything is fine," Karen said. "I dropped my dinner."

"We want no trouble."

"There is no trouble."

"OK, OK," he said, and Karen heard his footsteps creak on the stairwell.

Staring at the ceiling with its cracks and stains, she drifted off, so tired. She suddenly craved sleep. A long, dark sleep.

She shut her eyes.

The storm woke her up.

Rain battered the window and the glass buckled. Outside, trees whipped, and litter whirled as the wind tossed it around.

Karen got off the bed, went to the window.

It was wild out there. Pitch black. Maybe the power was out.

Lightning sliced the sky, illuminating everything for a second and what she saw made her gasp.

That wasn't the world she fell asleep in. It wasn't Earl's Court. It was a rocky terrain full of bubbling lakes of fire.

Then it was black again.

Her mind was playing tricks on her. She blinked, waited by the window for the next lightning flash.

Rain pelted the pane. Wind howled. Debris thrashed about.

The flash came.

The world was lit up again.

Karen screamed and staggered away from the window when the monstrous brute, bald-headed, covered in tattoos, wielding a lethal looking sickle, appeared right outside her room.

Darkness fell again. Thunder growled. A laugh, spiteful and horrific, echoed out of the night.

Karen shook. Her legs were like jelly. Her heart pounded and her belly was wheeling.

How was it possible that the psycho was at her third-floor window?

But he wasn't, was he. She was seeing things. Her mind playing tricks. Stress getting to her.

The window shattered, a sickle's crescent-shaped blade smashing through the glass.

Karen shrieked and flung herself across the room, stumbling towards the door.

And she just about managed to turn the knob and yank it open when a dark shadow filled the room behind her.

In the corridor, she froze.

Her eyes adjusted to the red-lit hallway.

This wasn't the hotel's corridor.

This was a passageway to Hell.

Blood seeped from the walls. Bones dangled from hooks attached to the ceiling. Body parts carpeted the floor.

There were heads, legs, arms, torsos littered along the corridor. The place stank of rotting flesh.

Karen stared at the hellish scene but strangely she wasn't scared.

In fact, she felt calm.

She breathed, taking in the odour of death and corruption that filled the air.

She could still hear the storm roar, and again, from the room behind her, she glanced at the lightning. Thunder followed seconds later. And after the thunder, from the static, that voice:

"Let me loose, Karen. Let the world feel my love."

She headed towards the voice, or towards where she thought it was coming from.

Carefully making her way past the mutilated body parts, avoiding the bones dangling from the ceiling, trying not to touch the blood-wet walls.

She turned the corner. The stairs were there, but they weren't the creaky old ones she'd climbed up when she booked in.

They were carpeted in what appeared to be human skin.

Depictions of torture and death had been scrawled onto the walls.

The voice came again, deep, guttural:

"Karen, bring me to the world. I will make you proud. I will show you the purity of hate. The clarity of pain. The glory of blood. The beauty of wounds. The rage of love."

She pursued the voice, desperate to find it.

The displays of horror she waded through didn't bother her at all.

Now she passed humans nailed to the walls, their naked bodies glistening with blood. They wailed and screamed, begging her to get them down.

But iron tent pegs had been driven through the crook of their elbows and through their kneecaps, pinning them to the walls.

The crucified were men, women—and children.

But Karen ignored their agony, their pleading.

The voice called her:

"I will kill for you, Karen, if you give birth to me. I will love you..."

Karen came to what appeared to be the centre of a maze, with four passageways leading off—including the one she had followed to get here.

There, on a pile of twisted, mutilated bodies, sat a huge, shadowy figure.

"... if you love me," it said.

It stood up. It was enormous—seven-feet tall. Karen craned her neck as it rose up from its fleshy throne. She couldn't see it properly, but she could smell it.

It smelled like a charnel house. Burning flesh, rotting meat. But to Karen's nostrils it was strangely sweet.

The giant raised its huge arm above its head. Brandished in its hand was the serrated-bladed sickle.

A lightning strike lit the cove, illuminating the figure.

Karen saw it clearly, and it saw her. Both screamed.

Karen screamed herself awake.

Daylight poured through the window.

It was sunny outside, no hint of the storm.

She scrabbled off the bed and went to the window. It wasn't shattered. She stared outside. The pavements were dry. The bins stood up in a neat line and weren't hurled about at all. Commuters trudged to work. Cars gridlocked the road. Horns blared as pissed off drivers expressed their frustration at being late for the office.

Karen grabbed her phone. Dead battery. Bollocks.

She blinked, and the figure with the sickle flashed in her mind. She gasped. Everything came back to her.

She looked at the door. Rushed towards it. Opened it. Looked outside.

Just a grubby corridor, the cleaner shoving her cart.

No bones hanging from the ceiling, no blood on the walls, no limbs on the floor.

But she knew it had been real. It had felt and smelled real. That world she'd experienced existed, she was sure of it.

She slammed the door shut, powered up her laptop, and began to write furiously. Her head was filled with what she'd dreamed—or imagined—the previous night. She poured it all on the page.

After a long time—she had no idea how long, but it was dark outside by then—she stopped. She'd written 25,000 words. She couldn't believe it.

She'd poured them out. Given birth to them. But she'd forgotten what she'd written. Had no idea what had come out of her, what she'd created. She scrolled back to the start of her manuscript and read:

Chapter One. Ironbones was born in a furnace of fury and chaos and hatred. A storm raged. Lightning tore at the fabric of the sky, its violent, bright forks providing a brief glimpse to the terrible world beyond this one. Crone lay in pools of her own fluid, and roared with—

TRUE LOVE AND PURE RAGE

12 months later...

"WHERE DID THE idea for Ironbones come from?" someone asked.

Karen, sporting a whole new look and a brand-new name, smiled. "Hell, I think."

The audience laughed. They were book nerds. Geeky goths. Horror and fantasy freaks. Faithful followers of Karen's—or Kaz Payne as she now called herself—blog, which she had started to write while working on Ironbones.

Now with short, crow-black hair, wearing leather and lace, she had hurled herself into a sub-culture she'd known little about.

Ironbones was being placed firmly into that world, and the novel was hitting the right notes.

It had started to attract a lot of attention from fans of horror—especially extreme horror. Karen found they were all very nice people, despite their love of brutality. She wasn't going to analyse them. She was a writer, not a therapist. All that mattered to her was that she was building an audience. And Ironbones had certainly captured the imagination.

Not bothering with traditional publishing, Karen had eventually decided to self-publish.

Ironbones: The First Cut would be her baby. No one would tell her "No" when she sent it off in the post. No one would tell her cut this, add that. No one would say change the whole thing. It was hers. Pure and simple. Ironbones was her offspring.

She even designed the cover, although it was crap. Just a sickle covered in blood.

She had plotted the marketing campaign too, pushing drafts of the book out to bloggers, vloggers, reviewers, fans with more than five-hundred followers on Twitter and Instagram. Anyone who used the hashtag #horror on social media. She put time and effort into this. She'd given everything and life had been put on hold.

But it didn't matter. The important thing was that Ironbones was being born, and what felt like true love and pure rage came together in Karen's heart.

The world was about to meet the character she felt was as real as any person in this room.

Reviews so far had been positive. The nerds, the geeks, the vloggers and bloggers had embraced Ironbones.

Word of mouth started to spread. Already by the time of the launch, the horror fraternity were speaking his name:

Ironbones...

She had heard it whispered at conferences, listened to it uttered in bars and book clubs, at bus stops.

"You heard of this Ironbones?"

"You seen Ironbones on Facebook?"

"This incredible serial killer."

"Cuts people up."

"Eats their faces off."

"Ironbones is coming."

Karen would smile to herself. Her flesh would ripple. Her heart would pound.

At the launch in a bookshop called House of Grind in Hoxton, East London—a store crammed with horror books, comics, paraphernalia, legal drugs—nearly one-hundred-and-fifty people had gathered. It was quite an achievement for a self-published book in a niche genre.

Karen was pleased. She scanned the audience. Waited for another question.

A man stood—mid-20s, thick beard, glasses, Motorhead T-shirt.

"Do you like it when Ironbones cuts babies in half?"

Karen flinched. The guy's stare was steady, cool. His head was tilted to one side, waiting for her answer. Demanding it in fact. He really wanted to know if she liked it when Ironbones cut babies in half.

"I'm not sure 'like' it is the correct expression," she said. "But Ironbones does what Ironbones does. I'm not justifying violence."

"You're saying violence is a beautiful thing, an art," the guy said.

Karen knitted her brow. "Am I?"

"He cuts babies in half—there's a scene in the book, or at least in the draft I read. Cuts a baby in two."

"Like Solomon suggested."

"But Ironbones does it."

"Yeah, he's a monster."

"You created him."

"I did."

"He's kind of your baby."

"He is."

"Thank you," the guy said, and sat down.

Karen rolled her eyes and smiled nervously at the host, Jack Sane, owner the House of Grind.

Sane said, "We'll move on. Let me ask you, Kaz, you suffered a lot of rejection during your career as a writer. There are many aspiring writers here this evening who find it difficult to get any kind of interest in their work. You've finally bitten the bullet and chosen to go it alone, self-publish. And so far, it's looking good. Do you have a message, first to the would-be authors out there, struggling with rejection, and second, to the publishers who said no, time after time, to your submissions?"

George Ellis tore open the package. It was black wrapping, matte finish. It was addressed to him at Parlour, his name typed out in Gothic font. There was no sender information. Ellis rarely opened mail. That's why he had Sophie. Unfortunately she'd gone home. Something about only working forty-hour weeks. Ungrateful little hussy. Off to fuck her boyfriend probably. She could have waited another hour to accept this package from the delivery man. Fucked him if she was horny.

But Ellis was on his own in the office. Working late as usual. Never home before ten. Always at his desk before eight. That's why Parlour was a success, and why Ellis had suffered two heart attacks and was on lisinopril for his high blood pressure, metformin for type 2 diabetes.

But what else did he have? No family. Just a passion for books. And the drive to succeed.

So when the bell rang, he had initially ignored it. But then he thought it might be the boy he'd ordered, although if so, he was early.

In any case, Ellis trundled down the two flights of stairs to the front door and opened it to a very tall man standing in the shadows, holding a package.

"For you, Mr Ellis," the huge man said, and backed away into the gloomy street—almost as if he were melting into the darkness itself.

Intrigued, Ellis returned upstairs to open the parcel. Inside was an envelope, black again, with his name on it in the same gothic-style font as the address.

The parcel also contained a book wrapped in cloth, as if it were some ancient volume requiring protection from the elements.

He unwrapped the cloth. Inside was a pulpy looking paperback with an image of a bloody sickle on the cover, and the title Ironbones: The First Cut written in a horror-style font.

The author was Kaz Payne—not a name Ellis was familiar with. And he couldn't imagine any reason why he'd been sent the book.

He furrowed his brow, thinking, trying to work out why? He opened the envelope and took out a letter, read it, his mouth agape:

Dear Mr Ellis, Some time ago you told me I had no talent. Thank you. Because the anger you kindled in me has resulted in this, my very first novel to be published, albeit self-published. But so far, readers have loved it. I hope you love it too. All the best, Karen Davies.

He chuckled. That bloody woman. Of course he remembered her. How could he forget? She'd pestered him for years, sending him her terrible novels. It was akin to stalking.

He studied the paperback. A five-by-eight with a glossy cover. He flicked through the pages. A strange smell came off them as a breeze whispered over his cheeks. He couldn't place the odour, but it was sweet; putrid.

It was a two-hundred-and-fifty-page novel. The inside cover page was signed by Karen Davies. Her message said, *Read it. I dare you—KD.*

Again he laughed to himself. Idiot girl, he thought.

Something creaked outside the office. He'd left the door ajar. Light came from the stairwell.

"Hello?" he said.

But then he dismissed the creak as nothing.

"Read, indeed," he said out loud, and he poured himself a brandy and went to the leather couch, sank into it, opened the page to chapter one.

Ellis flinched again.

Not for the first time.

He squirmed as if in pain.

Not for the first time.

He gasped with dread.

Not for the first time.

And he turned the page.

Not for the first time.

Because it was a page-turner, you had to give her that. He couldn't stop reading. He wanted to keep going. To look at the atrocities committed on virtually every page. It felt like driving slowly past a terrible accident. You wanted to see although you knew it was wrong. You knew what you were about to witness was going to be dreadful.

And it was. In so many ways. But also gripping. Just like a road accident.

He turned the page again.

Chapter thirteen. The last chapter according to the contents page. The chapter's was title:

It ends bloodily.

He gritted his teeth, fearing what he might read. Knowing it would make his stomach churn.

But on he went.

The office grew darker. It was past midnight. Ellis hadn't even noticed the time. Had he a wife or a husband or a mother, they might have called him and said, "George, it's nearly one in the morning. Where are you?" He might have looked at the clock and said, "Oh goodness, I had no idea. I'm on my way."

And he would have packed up and left. And lived.

But there was no one to call him. No one for him to call. No one to inspire him to pack up. If there were, he probably would have still been in one piece. Instead of pieces.

He read:

"The publisher slouched on the settee, his bulbous frame cascading on the leather..."

Bitch, he thought, writing about me.

He kept reading. The bulb in the early 20th century Kashmiri Table Lamp perched on the George III period mahogany tall whatnot shelf flickered.

Something creaked again on the stairwell. Ellis heard but didn't take any notice. He was engrossed. Or grossed out maybe.

But he read on.

His legs jerked. He suffered with Willis-Ekbom Disease, or restless leg syndrome, a sign of iron deficiency. Often it would be a sign that he needed to get some sleep.

But not tonight.

He needed to end this agony.

Finish this book.

This ugly, nasty little book that had gripped him.

He ploughed on, turning the pages as the lights flickered, as his legs twitched.

As darkness engulfed the room, he came to the last page.

The lamp went out. Ellis gasped. Looked up. The street-lights had gone out too. It was very dark.

A shadow, huge and ominous, passed in front of the window.

The shape of a man. The size of a giant.

"Who's that?" Ellis yelled. Bowels as well as legs twitching now.

He shuddered all over.

A figure seemed to form in the darkness.

"Who are you?" Ellis asked, his voice raspy, scared shitless.

The light of the moon caught metal. It drew Ellis's attention away from the actual size of the trespasser. The publisher was fixed on the vicious looking sickle with a serrated blade that the giant wielded in a hand the size of a Qianlong Blue & White dish from the 18th century, featuring a mountain scene with scholars on a bridge, that Ellis had recently bought for £600.

The plate was eleven inches in diameter.

Ellis couldn't stop staring at the hand brandishing the sickle, the moonlight glinting on the blade.

Then:

"She's good isn't she."

The voice was guttural, not human. As if it came through one of those voice changers that distorted your speech.

Then it said, "So good it's real."

The figure stepped forward. One step to cover the distance between Ellis and where the darkness lay. One step that would take five for a normal man.

Ellis screamed when he saw the trespasser. His size. His pale white flesh. The tattoos. The shaved skull. The red eyes. The smile that displayed black metal teeth, sharpened.

And the sickle.

Swinging up.

Slicing down.

Glinting.

Ellis wet himself. He dropped the book. Threw his arms up to protect himself.

Shrieked.

The blade cut through his forearms. Amputated them just below the elbow. They fell to the floor, fingers still twitching. Blood spurting.

Ellis screeched. Stared at his stumps, blood spouting from them. He couldn't fathom what had happened. Couldn't understand where his hands had gone, his fingers.

The blade rose again. Held high. Ready to hack.

Ellis looked up.

He tried to say something, his brain telling him it was Please don't kill me, but the message didn't reach his mouth. All that came out was some desperate yowling.

The monster said: "We don't always get what we want. Do we."

But not in its own voice. The voice of a woman. A voice Ellis recognized.

His mouth opened wide. But no sound was coming out now. Nothing was coming out of him only blood and shit.

The sickle slashed downwards. The blade went straight into Ellis's mouth. Sliced through teeth, tongue, gums, bone. Hacked and got stuck in the alveolar process.

The point of the blade protruded from Ellis's throat. His eyes were wide, a man who couldn't understand what was happening to him.

And then blood started to spurt copiously, and he made a strange animal noise: prey in agony.

But he still wasn't dead. It took him a while to die. His killer was an expert at keeping victims alive. At inflicting as much agony as was possible. And Ellis felt all of it.

The detective constable said, "Secretary found him this morning, 7:30 am." He checked his notes. "Name of Sophie Kapinski."

"Shagging?" said Detective Inspector John Drake, eyes on the catastrophe in George Ellis's office.

"Gay," said the DC. "Ellis that is. Don't know about the secretary. Sort of hope she isn't. Know what I mean, boss?"

"Where was the girl? Secretary."

"Home, she says."

"Where is she now?"

"Hospital. Sedated. Right state. Found him. Like this."

"Like this" was dismembered. Blood everywhere; guts too. Carpet a marshy swamp. Gore splashed all over the walls and the antique stuff that Ellis must've spent thousands accumulating. The publisher had been sliced open from chin to his sternum by what the coroner initially had suggested was a saw. But he'd have to wait for the post-mortem examination, he told Drake. State of Ellis, it seemed the poor sod had already gone through a post-mortem examination—while he was still alive.

"Big strong man," the coroner had said. "Takes immense strength to slice through bone and sinew like that."

After sawing, the killer or killers had wrenched Ellis's chest wide open, snapping ribs.

"Hugely strong man," the coroner had said.

Ellis' heart and lungs had been removed and placed on his desk in some atrocious take on a flower arrangement.

Then his entrails had been yanked out and now lay in a steaming pile on the carpet.

The entire digestive tract from mouth to anus, twenty feet of human organ, had been removed and draped on the Victorian double scroll end settee.

Ellis's forearms had been cut off just below the elbow and they'd been placed, like pencils, in a vase on the table.

His legs had been hacked off at the thighs and placed on his chair as if they were sitting there, without an upper body.

The killer, or killers, had nailed the legs to the chair with tent pegs to make sure they stayed put, didn't slide off.

He—or they —were serious and meticulous about what they were doing.

The place reeked of death.

"Fucking sick," the DC said, more to himself that to Drake.

A forensics officer came up to Drake with a plastic evidence bag containing a paperback book stained in blood.

"He was reading this," the chap said, handing Drake the bag.

Drake held it up and peered at the book. "What's it called? Can't see for all the blood."

Karen read the news of George Ellis's death on the BBC website at 10:00 am.

She was sitting at her kitchen table eating toast and drinking instant coffee.

She was tired. It had been a long night. The launch party had gone on till 3:00 am.

And she'd been there till 3:00 am, too. With loads of people who could all confirm her presence at the Hoxton bookstore.

She never left officer. She was here from 8:00 pm.

And when she did leave, she left with loads of people. And brought them home. To party some more. Till 5:30 am. They took photos on their phone, which were time stamped. Photos of her. Selfies with her. She was the host.

Always present, officer. That's right. Never left.

It was 9:30 am when the last of her guests went home. He was the editor of a horror website who she sucked off. She let him sleep in her bed, too.

Next to her the whole time, officer.

Then she was alone. And she read about Ellis's death. Not much info, other than he'd been found in his office by his secretary.

But it was murder, they said.

They were questioning "a man in his early twenties", the website reported.

She raised her eyebrows.

At 10:30 am the doorbell rang—two detectives.

"So you can account for your movements, and provide witnesses to confirm all of that, from 8:00 pm last night to just over an hour ago?" the top cop called John Drake asked while the other one, a detective constable, took notes.

"I can." She fluttered her eyelashes at him. She was a bit dazed. Lack of sleep, too much wine. She felt edgy too. Fatigue does that to you. Drake, a DI, was a handsome bastard, and Karen had a soft spot for handsome bastards. You know the sort: dashing, glint in the eye. She said, "Who's this man your questioning."

He looked at her, and his eyes narrowed. Handsome bastard. Hesitated before saying, "Escort Ellis had..."

"Ordered?"

"I suppose."

"He did it, you think?"

Handsome bastard didn't answer. Glanced around the flat. Said, "How long have you lived here?"

"Nine months or so."

"You lived in a hotel?"

"Earl's Court, right. Checked up on me, then."

He made a sort of "of course we have" gesture with his head. He was about forty, maybe. Brown eyes that just swallowed you. Dark hair neatly cropped. Flecks of silver in it. He was lean, looked after himself. And his suit was expensive. Good shoes too. Her imagination started to grind. Her fingers twitched. She wanted to get back to work, revising her next Ironbones book—and as from now, something had to change.

"Why did you move?" he asked.

They were sitting in the lounge. Her flat was a one-bedroom in Peckham. Affordable but nothing grand. Part of a refurbished tower block.

"Why wouldn't I?"

She sipped coffee. She ran a hand through her hair. She knew what was coming.

"You've got a charge for common assault, Miss Davies."

"I do." She chuckled: I do. Sounded as if she was answering the "Do you take this man?" question.

"What's funny?"

She shook her head. "Sorry, knackered."

His eyes narrowed. Sexy beast, she thought.

Then he asked, "You've a propensity to violence?"

"Don't we all?"

"Do we?"

"We're chimps."

"What?"

"Chimps," she repeated. "Evolutionarily, we're chimps."

"OK."

"Chimps go to war."

He nodded.

She shrugged. Repeated, "We're chimps."

He said, "So it's justifiable what you did? And what happened to George Ellis?"

"It's not about justifiable. Justifiable is not nature. Personally, I'm sorry it happened. Connie and Mr Ellis. I fell out with Connie. I was very stressed at the time, did a terrible thing, paid for it. Regards Mr Ellis, well, I'll be honest, he was mean to me sometime ago. But that's publishing. I moved on. Now look at me?"

He did—for a good long while. Said, "You had a massive ruck with him, according to his secretary. Threw a chair."

She raised her eyebrows and smiled. "I'm feisty."

"Was it because he was mean to you, then?"

She shrugged: a sort of "yes".

"What did he say to you?"

"Just gave a book I'd written a bad review. I lost my shit. Was under a lot of strain back then. OK now, though. Don't you reckon?"

The way he looked her up and down, he did reckon.

Then he stood. She did too. His DC caught up, stood as well, flustered like the third wheel always is.

"Thanks for your time," said handsome bastard.

"Anything else?" she said.

"You're not leaving the country, are you?" he asked, hint of a grin.

"Why, will you miss me?" she said. Hint of a grin.

After handsome-bastard cop left, Karen opened her laptop at the kitchen table and went to the Ironbones file.

Book two was almost done. Or it had been. She'd been looking out for a hero. You know how the song goes.

Well, a nemesis, really. For Ironbones.

The first book had seen him butcher mostly teenagers. It was just like a slasher movie—a slasher novel.

Critics had liked that. Many, of course, had read more into it. They'd argued that it was a comment on slasher movies, and ironic in many ways. The violence was a metaphor for the intellectual violence perpetrated against the iGen and millennial generations.

Karen thought: What a load of bollocks. But if those wankers wanted to see it like that, fine.

She stared at the manuscript on screen:

Ironbones: God of Carnage.

She started to read.

She'd introduced a copper in book one. A detective called Allport. A useless, uncharismatic buffoon who died nastily at the end.

Book two's cop was another two-dimensional type, a flash harry called Curtis. But Curtis, like Allport, was no match for Ironbones. She needed a strong antagonist.

So Gabriel Messenger was born. John Drake by another name.

She spent the day rewriting, replotting, and finally, Ironbones had a worthy adversary.

A cop to catch a killer.

The Sun's headline screamed:

BRUTAL KILLER HACKS PUBLISHER TO DEATH

Robert Gilchrist carefully cut it out.

He pinned it to the corkboard on his bedroom wall.

"Dinner, darling," came the tiny little voice from downstairs.

Gilchrist said nothing. Went back to his desk where his computer hummed. He opened the Word document. Leaned back in his chair and pondered. Reached up to casually drift his hand through the hanging mobiles dangling from his ceiling.

But they weren't really mobiles.

They jangled as he ran his hand through them. Metal clinking against metal.

Axes clinking against daggers.

Hammers clinking against sickles.

He liked doing that. The sound chilled him out.

"Dinner, darling," came the voice again.

He ignored it and leaned his portly frame forward, started to type.

Someone tapped gently on the door.

"Dinner, darling," came the quiet little voice from outside the door.

"Fuck off, Mother!!" he shrieked.

"Strange letter," said DI John Drake.

He was standing in an office in CID at Church Street police station in Marylebone, in the borough of Westminster—the local cop shop when it came to St John's Wood, where George Ellis had been murdered.

Karen stood right next to Drake. Gazing up at him. Imagining him to be —

"DI Messenger, why do you think they wrote to me?"

"It's DI Drake," he said.

Karen blushed. "Sorry, of course."

"Who's DI Messenger?"

"My hero."

She sat. Crossed her legs in tight black jeans.

"Hero?"

"Character in my new book. Ironbones's nemesis."

He looked at her, really studying her. Then he looked at the letter. It had been signed by someone calling themselves

Offspring

Declared Karen to be their

Mother

The one who'd given birth to him, allowed him to live and breathe.

The letter thanked her for giving him life, freeing him to find himself by spilling blood.

Drake said, "This is a copy. Our techies have the original. They're running tests."

"You think it's him?" she asked. "The one who killed Ellis?"

"Hard to tell. Nothing there that isn't in the public domain. No information that we could say came from the killer. Thank you for bringing it in. You will let me know if you hear any more from this individual, or anyone else who's—you know—a little weird."

She got up, wiggled in her tight black jeans.

"Everyone who reads my book is a little weird, Mr Drake."

He hesitated. Then:

"Call me John," he said, in a voice that sounded as if he'd made a life-changing decision, an *I'm-giving-up-my-well-paid-job-and-going-back-packing-around-the-world* kind of decision.

"All right," she said, and tested it on her tongue: "John."

"Please don't make this letter public, though. Some people just want attention. Do this kind of thing all the time. They'll come forward, say they're the killer when they're patently not."

She fluttered her eyelashes. "Patently?"

He smiled a shy smile, said, "To be honest, this is likely nothing. Just a nutcase. Don't quote me on that though. Saying 'nutcase'. It's not a technical term. But better safe than sorry."

"That's why you should always wear a condom, DI John," she said.

There was a moment of silence and staring at each other.

He broke it, saying, "Before you go..."

He tailed off. Was he going to ask her out?

"Do you mind if we could take a look at the manuscript for your latest book?"

Her shoulders slumped. "Why?"

"It might offer clues."

"To what?"

"To Ellis's murder."

"How? I'm the only one to have seen the manuscript so far. No one else."

"Might help. May be something in there, you never know. Give us a heads up if something else happens."

"You reckon something else will happen?"

"This wasn't a one-off, Miss Davies."

"Karen."

"Karen," he said—not like he was trying it out on his tongue at all. "This was not a crime of passion. Not done in anger. This was meticulous. A slow, brutal dismembering by a perpetrator who seemed to enjoy what he was doing."

"Or she."

"Or she, yes. But more likely a he. Killer was immensely strong."

"So men are stronger than women?"

"Generally, whether you like it or not."

She pouted. "I feel a bit micro-aggressed, Gabriel."

"John."

Drake flinched again, digging his nails into the arm of the chair.

"Jesus-fucking-wept," he said.

He was sitting on the couch at his flat near Victoria where he'd been reading a typed manuscript of Ironbones: God of Carnage for the past two hours.

It was 9:00 pm now. He had about a hundred pages to go. The novel was brutal. The cover said it was

A no-holds barred work of extreme horror.

The cover was right. So you can judge some books by their covers

The protagonist, if he could be called that, was an out-of-control monster with a quick wit and a sharp sickle.

He would appear from nowhere and start hunting down a bunch of people—teenagers at a hostel, holidaymakers at a hotel, office workers on an away day—and one by one cut them to pieces.

There had been a bit in the middle when it seemed the hero cop Gabriel Messenger had the upper hand, but it turned out he hadn't.

Drake had predicted that near the end there'd be a scene which was supposed to convince you that this beast, this Ironbones, had been killed by Messenger.

Karen Davies—or Kaz Payne, her pseudonym—had called Drake that during their interview. Mistaken him for this character.

Messenger hadn't appeared in the first book. The first book, which colleagues had read, featured a fat, useless copper, who got sawn in half at the end.

Drake had now just read the scene where Ironbones died—although with many pages left in the novel, it wasn't a long shot to bet he'd be back.

The killer had been crushed under a collapsing office building. Messenger was stood near the rubble with the naturally sexy secretary he'd saved from the monster's clutches.

She was your "last girl". A horror-movie trope. The final surviving female. Ripley in Alien was the original. Now they were all over the place.

The book was easy to read. It wouldn't be Drake's literature of choice. He enjoyed thrillers by the likes of Michael Connelly and the Irish writer Ken Bruen, though the latter got police procedure so wrong it was laughable.

Horror certainly wasn't his thing, but there was something gripping about this trash.

Definitely made you want to read. Stupid, though: a seven-foot killer forged in a furnace of hate and fury, born during a storm to a mother called Crone, a witch-like creature who mated with demons—or so she imagined. She was mad and was locked up in an asylum.

He continued reading. Bracing himself for the inevitable horror that was to come.

Tommy Wallis smacked Nadim Abdi right in the face.

"It's fucking my turn," Wallis said, prowling towards the decked boy.

Abdi held on to the book. He also held on to his nose. It was gushing blood. His eyes watered. It felt as if his face was on fire.

As Wallis rushed towards him, he scuttled away using his feet. Getting purchase on the tarmac was hard. But he was in survival mode.

He got to his feet and retreated as Wallis approached.

"Give it to me," Wallis said, face twisted in fury.

"It's my go," Abdi said, his voice muffled due to his broken nose.

He wasn't much of a fighter. But he'd fight for this. The book had been doing the rounds. All the Year 8s at Hadleigh High School in Southend, Essex, had read it. Or so they said. All of them apart from Abdi. And Wallis.

He was the class bully. He was big for his age with big fists and big shoulders. He'd smacked Abdi before, but then Wallis had smacked a lot of people.

"Leave him alone, Wallis, you can't even read," said Mackenzie Shipman, a blond girl who all the boys fancied.

Abdi looked at her with awe. She'd defended him. The prettiest girl in Year 8 had said to leave him alone.

"Shut up, slag," said Wallis.

"Don't you fuckin' call me a slag, you fat cunt," spat Shipman.

Abdi gasped. Such venom pouring from such beauty.

Shipman even squared up to the bully and slapped him across the face.

The rest of the kids went

Ohhhh...

There was a crowd of them. Most of Year 8 by the looks of things. And a few older kids too.

Wallis reeled.

Would he hit a girl? Big question.

Answer was yes.

He spun round to face Shipman, who was much smaller than him. Drew back his fist. She gawped, not believing he'd do it.

Abdi flew at him. Lunged and swung his fists at the bully's head. Cracked Wallis with punch after punch.

The bully screeched and reeled away. He fell on his arse. The crowd laughed.

Abdi looked at Shipman and she looked back.

Abdi felt very hot and sensed his face had gone very red. His mouth was dry. He looked at the book:

Ironbones: God of Carnage

Tattered copy. Read so often, by so many, the pages were coming loose. And it wasn't an old book, either. Came out just a few weeks ago.

He wasn't supposed to have it. Mum and Dad had warned him against it. Heard about other kids reading it. Mum and Dad were going to kill him. But he didn't care. He wanted to read this book. He wanted to impress Mackenzie Shipman.

Laughter still filled the air around him, everyone mocking Wallis.

And then a voice boomed:

"What on earth is going here?"

William Merson, deputy head teacher at Hadleigh High School, said, "This book is filth. It's a disgrace. Finding it in the hands of thirteen- and fourteen-year-old children was akin to finding drugs on their persons. It made me sick."

Karen stood in her flat watching the TV. She was tapping her foot. Biting her nails. Couldn't sit down. She was so wound up.

The teacher, floppy hair, round glasses, looked old before his time. He was really enjoying his moment in the sun, though he had a face like an old shoe.

"I'm of the view that such books should be banned. But this won't happen, of course. That's the world. Freedom of expression and all that liberal nonsense. But if children—young people—get a hold of this sort of mind-warping filth, this sort of debased, degrading material, the authors should bear some responsibility. This woman"—he really spat that word out: woman, like he hated the bloody things or something; like they should be in the kitchen—"ought to be punished for this abomination, which is not only a plague on our children, but an insult to our lord and saviour Jesus Christ."

"Punished, you reckon," Karen said to the TV, which now cut to a middle-aged woman with short red hair.

"While we are very concerned that there was an incident at the school," said the woman, named on screen as Carol Hedges, headmistress, "we don't want to discourage reading. Of course, some material is unsuitable for children. Also, we don't hold with Mr Merson's argument that an author should be punished. He does not speak for the school in this matter, but he does have a right to his opinion, and we sympathise with his concerns."

They cut back to Merson.

"I'm sorry that neither the school nor the local authority has backed me in this matter. I will, naturally, continue to work at Hadleigh High. I have a duty to the children. But I will now be aiming to put a stop to filth like this."

He held up a copy of the book. Tattered and dog-eared.

Then, like a magician whipping out a rabbit from inside his coat, he made appear another book, Ironbones: The First Cut. Again tattered and dog-eared.

He said, "She's written two of the hellish things."

The reporter's voiceover said, "A few parents have supported Mr Merson's stance."

They cut to a scene in a back garden where a group of Muslims, plus a few non-Muslims, tossed copies of both novels on a bonfire.

A white man with an orange beard, wearing a taqiyah—the skullcap worn by Muslim males—was speaking now. He was named on screen as *Malcom Wilson, parent,* and he said, "We fully support Mr Merson's stance. We may follow a different religion—he is a Christian—but it seems that only people of faith truly have any morals these days. If our children can get their hands on such filth so easily, we can't stand by and allow it to happen."

Merson then came into the garden. Karen rolled her eyes: what a set-up. The deputy head was greeted like a prophet by the gathered all-sorts. Karen said, "Cunt."

The teacher was carrying a ruck sack. He emptied its contents on the grass. Copies of Ironbones: The First Cut and Ironbones: God of Carnage.

Kids and adults led by Merson and Wilson started hurling the book on the bonfire.

The flames crackled and danced like an animal being fed.

Karen didn't know whether to laugh or cry.

If Karen had an agent, or a publisher, they might have told her the hoopla over her book being the subject of a fight between Year 8 pupils was good publicity.

They would have said,

Ride the storm.

They would have said,

Keep a dignified silence.

They would have organised other authors and prominent people to condemn the book burning.

But Karen had no one.

Only Ironbones.

The following morning, she went to the shop and saw the newspaper headlines:

BAN THIS BOOK!

screamed a tabloid, with a photo of the teacher, Merson, staged, on the front page showing him dumping copies of Ironbones: God of Carnage into a black dustbin sack.

So if she'd had an agent or a publisher, they would have said to her, Someone's buying all these books, so that's a good thing.

But it didn't feel good right now, watching people burn your books, tossing them it into dustbin sacks.

Karen felt something cold crawl up her spinal cord, and a voice in her head whispered something inaudible at first, but which became clearer the more she read:

Cut them down... cut them down... the voice seemed to be whispering.

She pulled the papers off the shelf, laid them on the floor, started to scour them.

Apart from the tabloid, most nationals had an item on the inside pages. The Guardian, though, had a photo of the book burning on the front page.

The Evening Standard went with

KIDS RIOT OVER HORROR NOVEL

as its main headline. The book burning was mentioned on the turn, on page four. Merson was quoted, vilifying Karen's writing, claiming it was "turgid, amateurish and no better than a five-year-old's early scribblings".

The Daily Mail had

PARENTS FURY OVER "SICK" HORROR NOVEL THAT CAUSED SCHOOLYARD BRAWL

The Daily Star broke the mould, went with:

MY HUSBAND MARRIED A CABBAGE

She boiled with indignation. Something deep inside her was coming apart: the cords that held her together.

"You buying those or what?"

She turned. The shopkeeper scowled at her. She held his gaze. He looked away and mumbled something about this not being a library, you know.

Karen scooped up the pile of papers. She went to the counter. Fixed eyes with the shopkeeper again.

He must've seen something in her look that made him hesitate, because you could see him rear back slightly.

Who knows what he saw? Maybe something darker than he'd ever seen before, something that inspired awe—and fear.

She grabbed a packet of Haribo and slapped them on the counter.

"That too," she said.

He mumbled again. Took the twenty-pound note she tossed at him. Gave her the change. Breathed a sigh of relief when she stormed out of the shop.

It would take her an hour and a half to get to Southend. Overground service from Peckham Rye, disembarking at Canada Water. A Jubilee Line tube service to West Ham. Then a 45-minute journey on the train operator c2c to Southend Central.

For most people, it would be enough time to calm down.

For Karen it was enough time to get that molten rock inside her to maximum temperature.

She'd stare out of the window the entire journey, but not remember one thing she saw—just silently cursing Merson the whole way.

Telling herself she'd teach him a lesson. How dare he tell her she couldn't write.

"You've seen what happens to people who piss me off," she'd tell him.

After checking the route, she shut the computer. Sat back in her chair.

No need for me to go anywhere, she thought. I'll stay right here. Make a call.

"Hi, John," she said, "it's Karen—"

"I know," he said, voice so deep, so manly. "Everything all right?"

"No..."

It's good to talk, she thought. And talked.

William Merson shut his briefcase and sat behind his desk in the empty classroom. Sat for a few seconds, breathing.

He felt light-headed. It had been a difficult few days. The fuss over the book had brought the school some unwanted attention. That heathen headmistress, Hedges, was angry with him. They'd had a confrontation that morning.

She had praised him for stopping the brawl in the playground, but bizarrely criticised him for pinpointing the reason for that brawl—the book.

It was a disgusting thing. He hadn't read it, obviously—never would. But he'd scoured the internet for reviews and extracts in between searches for TEEN SEX VIDEOS.

The troubled and the warped praised it, naturally. Hailed its thrills, its page-turning attributes, basked in the violence. It was a book full of cursing and blasphemy, no doubt. The idea itself of a supernatural being was an affront to God, who was the only supernatural being.

Apart from Satan. And Satan had surely played a part in this. It was time people opened their eyes. Time to make a stand.

For too long Merson's faith had been closeted, especially at the school.

It was obviously multi-faith and no faith, and he wasn't allowed to preach. He wasn't allowed to save the children's souls.

But Jesus said in Mark's Gospel,

Go ye into all the world, and preach the gospel to every creature so it was very difficult for Merson not to obey. He did it in his own way, obviously. He would start every class with a prayer—not a public one, just a display of personal faith. It might impress on some of the children the importance of worshipping God.

None had complained. They tittered. Some would ask him what he was doing. But he wasn't allowed to tell them. He would say, "Taking a moment to reflect and give thanks."

The kids would ask, "Thanks to who?"

He'd say, "Whom," which would divert the conversation towards grammar, conveniently, then led them on to whichever book or play they were studying.

It angered Merson, however. The lack of faith. The mocking of religion. He'd shake with rage and inwardly pray to God, asking forgiveness.

There had been an occasion when he started leaving Bible tracts in pupils' homework, and again Hedges stepped in.

This morning she had berated him for appearing on television yet again without the school's consent.

"I was speaking as a private citizen," he'd said.

"No, you cited school matters and your responsibilities as a teacher, William," Hedges said. "And for you to even be near those people who were burning the books, well, it's a disciplinary matter. The governors won't be happy."

They'll be split, Merson had thought, knowing many brothers and sisters in Christ sat on the school board, as well as good, decent Muslims who backed his stance.

Often, he'd pondered quitting Hadleigh High, find employment with perhaps an Academy school that taught Christian values.

But he never bit the bullet. He was too comfortable. Too frightened by change, maybe. He stayed put. At least he was deputy head now. And soon he'd be headmaster.

Hedges was on the look out for a new challenge, apparently. Other schools in Essex, troubled ones, had their eyes on her. For some reason she was regarded as some kind of "super head". Those who were parachuted into problem schools to sort them out. To be fair, she had sorted Hadleigh High out.

More luck than judgment, Merson thought.

He dropped to his knees behind his desk and clasped his hands together.

"Lord," he said. "Father in Heaven. Darkness seems to be everywhere these days. I'm surrounded by it. Satan's minions accost me. But you send me brothers from those of other faiths to support me. Thank you, Lord. Perhaps you need me to bring them to you too. This is why you took me to the burning. Tell me where to start, Father Jesus. Show me the way. Let me be your blade –"

Merson shivered. The temperature had suddenly plummeted. He opened his eyes. It had grown darker in the classroom. He glanced outside. The sky was slate grey. He looked at his watch. Barely gone 4:00 pm. Shouldn't be this gloomy. Was there a storm coming?

He got to his feet. His bones rattled with cold. He smelled something and stood still, not moving an inch. He sniffed—a sweet smell, unpleasant, made his stomach roil.

A strange green light shimmered under the stockroom door. Smoke, or maybe steam, seeped from under the door.

Merson stared, confused. His legs felt weak. His back was sweaty. That smell made him sick. Then a noise came from the stockroom. A guttural chuckle.

"Who's there?" asked the deputy head, his voice cracking.

He hesitated. Everything seemed very quiet and very still—a moment of true tranquillity.

The stockroom door exploded. Wood splintered and sprayed the classroom Uzi-style. The green light poured out. Filled the room with the reek of dead flesh.

Merson doubled up and retched.

And when the huge dark figure stepped out of the stockroom, he pissed himself.

The interloper was more than seven feet tall. The giant wore a leather waistcoat. Ripped jeans. Big cowboy boots stained red. Its arms were corded with muscles and covered in tattoos, as were its face and bald head. The tattoos seemed to be alive. Snakes writhing, dragons breathing fire, demons flapping their leathery wings. Beneath the tattoos, the stranger's flesh was sickly white.

And the fist gripping the sickle was the size of Merson's head.

The creature smiled at him, and the smile made Merson tremble. Its teeth were black and filed into sharp points.

The monster said, "You've been a bad boy, Willie. And you know what happens to bad boys."

Merson whimpered.

"Telling porkies about how moral you've been while jerking off over teen girls being fucked by dirty old men."

Merson's legs gave out. He made a yowling noise as they buckled under him. He was cowering now, on his knees again—but before a different god this time.

He didn't move when this god raised its sickle and brought it whizzing down.

The blade went through Merson's hand, pinning it to the desk. Initially he didn't feel any pain. He just stared for a brief second at the strange sight of steel piercing his flesh and the desk.

Then fire surged up his arm. He shrieked. Tried to get up, but he was stuck.

The monster loomed.

So much taller than Merson, so much stronger. He shrieked again—short, sharp, terrified

The monster grinned. Came face to face with the teacher. Moved in as for a kiss. Bit Merson's cheek off from jawline to temple.

A LOVE INTEREST

"KIDS FOUND HIM like this?"

Drake was appalled. On so many levels. To think children found their teacher nailed to the classroom wall, naked, castrated, gutted, both cheeks bitten off, was shocking to the detective. It would take years of therapy for those youngsters to deal with what they'd seen.

He was also personally appalled that another brutal killing had happened on his watch. This was out of his jurisdiction, but clearly linked to the slaughter of George Ellis months previously. Still unsolved, he thought, grimacing.

He would have to co-operate with Essex Police on Merson's murder. Too many cooks, he told himself.

But one good thing: he could see Karen Davies again.

He'd been talking to her when this happened. He pondered her—that seductive smile, the dark eyes. He liked her hair short like it was these days having seen photos of her on her Facebook page of how she looked before—princess blonde, princess pretty, princess spoilt.

She ditched all that. Was it due to her struggles as a writer? The perfect ten look got her nowhere. She went leftfield and hit the jackpot. Or at least got a foot on the rung of the ladder.

Her books were doing well. And now they would do even better. Linked to another murder.

The school had been shut for the day. The classroom where Merson had been discovered cordoned off. The place teemed with forensic officers. They had prised the tent pegs out of the teacher's feet and dropped them into evidence bags. Prised them out of his arms. Caught his remains as they virtually slithered off the wall. Basically, Merson was just a lump of gore.

The officers in their Tyvek suits looked liked Moomins, those strange kids TV creatures, to Drake. But this wasn't the scene of a kids TV show.

More like Saw, one of those torture porn movies.

Or torture porn literature like Ironbones: The First Cut and its sequel, which Drake had read.

He was standing outside the class with a sergeant from Essex Police. They were looking through the door, standing at the POLICE DO NOT ENTER ribbon.

"Yes, sir," the sergeant said, answering Drake's question about the kids finding Merson. "Traumatic for them. They're all with specialist officers, now. Social workers too, hopefully."

"Hopefully?"

She shrugged. "Funding. Psychologist on the way, too."

"Just one?"

She shrugged again. "Funding." The sergeant shook her head. "Never seen anything like this before. Have you, sir?"

He thought of Ellis. He felt sick. Not because of the appalling nature of the crimes. But because they appeared unsolvable. No clues. But a motive for sure—criticism of the books and the author.

Both victims had slammed Karen's work. This guy Merson had gone so far as to burn it. And look at him now?

They were still trying to trace whoever wrote the so-called "Offspring" letter to Karen, although Drake wasn't sure if the correspondent and the killer were one and the same.

Something about it didn't make sense, despite some other senior officers insisting they were the same person.

A copper came down the corridor and said, "That writer bird's here, inspector."

The sergeant said, "Less of the 'bird', constable."

Karen turned on the waterworks.

She and Drake sat at a table in the empty school canteen. He'd got her coffee. Made it with his own fair hands in the industrial-sized kitchen. Somehow found everything he needed, and probably broke some health & safety regulations and union rules in the process.

But he impressed her. He was impressive. He was everything a hero should be. Which is why he was her hero. But heroes didn't always survive. Heroes sometimes died, too.

She was wearing a black jumper dress from Topshop and flat shoes. Just enough cute to appeal. Just enough sexy.

She said, "Do you have any idea who might have done this?"

He sat back. Looked as if he was going to give her some bad news, said, "I have to ask you this, but where were you yesterday between 4:00 pm and 9:00 pm?"

She looked at him, smiled. Her eyes were damp. She fished in her pockets for something to wipe them with. He came up trumps again, finding serviettes. She trembled at that. Something primal in her shifting. As if he'd killed prey for her, brought meat to the entrance of her cave.

After shoving cavewoman back in her hollow, she told him where she was. At home with a few of friends. She made a show of trawling through her phone. Gave him a couple of numbers. Insisted as he was saying, no, no, it's fine. Telling him it's important, and that she understood that he had to ask her questions. Realized that she was embroiled in this investigation.

He hesitated, then:

"You reckon you're embroiled?"

"Someone is killing people who are saying nasty things about my book."

"I wouldn't say you, personally, are embroiled. You've been dragged into it, maybe, but..." He tailed off and shrugged.

"I think you're trying to protect me, DI Drake."

"John."

"John, yes."

"How do you mean?"

They were looking straight at each other's faces. Dead into one another's eyes. Fixed on each other's souls. And Karen was a pathogen, infecting him.

"You know," she said, all coy, "protecting me from all the bad press, from the blood and guts and terrible things. I am at the centre of this. It can't be helped. I understand completely that I have to be questioned. I'm on your wall, aren't I?"

"My wall?"

"Yes. Don't detectives have walls with material related to a murder investigation pinned to it?"

He smiled. "No we don't. It's all done on computer. No wall."

"Shit. Never mind. Perception is the most important thing. If it looks right, it is right."

"Your detective's got a wall?"

"He's got a wall."

She'd come up by train, so he drove her back.

He kept looking at her. Just checking to see if she was OK, he'd say. But he would say that, wouldn't he?

He fancies me, she thought.

Something fizzed in her belly. She knew it was going to happen. And when you know it was going to happen, it jazzed your biology.

She could picture it occurring—some hotel room, sweaty bodies fucking.

How was she going to write that?

Because Gabriel Messenger did need a love interest. He'd bed up with the daughter of one of the victims. A twentysomething journalist perhaps. They'd fall for each other, fall into bed with each other. Karen would write that into book three, Ironbones: Blood Will Be Everywhere, which she was working on

Then the fourth book, Messenger may have had had enough of life in the fast-lane and was thinking of calling it quits. Spend the rest of his life in a croft in the Scottish Highlands with this girl. But then Ironbones butchers her.

Cuts her open and rips from her belly the baby she was carrying—Messenger's baby.

Karen chuckled.

"You OK?" asked Drake.

"Yes, sorry."

He had his stern face on—as if he were berating her silently for laughing at this terrible time.

"What were you thinking about?"

"Next book."

"You find it easy to come up with ideas?"

"Yes, my imagination is always on the go. It's like a cauldron, bubbling with—you know—a casserole of ideas."

"And you imagine those deaths? They way Ironbones kills those people in the books?"

"Yes, of course I imagine them. I wrote them."

"Where does that come from? Such a pretty head." Bit of a smile now.

"It just comes. I don't curb my creativity. Don't put a leash on it. Look at the world. It's far worse than what I can come up with. People have invented cruelties beyond what I can think of. Beyond what Ironbones could inflict."

They hit some congestion on the A13, Stanford-le-Hope bypass. Construction work slowing traffic.

Karen didn't care. Neither did Drake by the looks of things. None of the usual sighing and guffawing you get when someone goes headlong into gridlock.

"There's certainly a violent perpetrator out there ," said Drake when the car had come to a complete stop in traffic. "I've never seen brutality like that before. Never witnessed anything as ferocious. And whoever did it, was displaying it."

"Like art."

"Not quite. But in his head, maybe yes"

"You still think it's a he?"

"Most killers are. The vast majority. Men murder, women destroy reputations."

"Is that true?"

"Basic psychology."

"So this is a man?"

"The strength to do what he's done suggests that beyond any psychology involved. Physically monumental. Bit like your character."

She said nothing. Traffic crawled.

"I'm violent," she said after a while.

He glanced at her, a question in his raised eyebrows.

She said, "I attacked Connie, didn't I."

He looked ahead, shuffled in his seat.

"That make you uncomfortable, John? Being around someone who could inflict such violence on another person?"

"I've been around a lot of violent people, and I can safely say, Karen, you don't strike me as cruel. I'm sure there were reasons for what you did. An aberration. You've not done it again, have you? No desire to, either?"

The traffic started to shift a little.

She put a hand on his thigh, said, "There's a hotel if you go right at this roundabout."

Without saying a word, he swung the car and took the last exit off the roundabout.

UNSOLVED

THE STIFFORD HALL HOTEL, Thurrock. An 18th century Georgian mansion set in six acres of parkland. Steeped in history. Friendly and efficient staff. Set in a picturesque village.

But none of that made Karen and Drake go, This sounds like a great place to fuck. They could have been in a tent in the middle of nowhere. Or a council flat in Hackney.

They were holed up in a room. They were celebrating. Or they were supposed to be celebrating.

Six years since they pulled off the A13 and parked up, without a word. Six years since they got out of the car silently, strolled to the hotel and asked for a room for the night.

Six years a couple.

They came to Stifford Hall every year on their anniversary. They could have afforded a better hotel, by now—or Karen could have—but it wasn't about money.

Drake was sitting at the desk, reading a newspaper.

From the shower Karen said, "They should learn to keep their mouths shut."

Drake looked up from the article. The headline read:

CRITIC OF VICIOUS HORROR NOVEL BUTCHERED AS "IRONBONES" KILLINGS REMAIN UNSOLVED

Drake cringed. Unsolved. Partly due to him. For eighteen months after the first murder until the day he was forced to quit the Met when his involvement with Karen became public knowledge, he'd got nowhere. No clues, no suspect.

During that time, twelve people were slaughtered. All twelve had criticised Karen's novels, or Karen personally.

It was a cause celebre. And it had fuelled an interest in the novels. The murders—from Ellis's to Merson's, and beyond—had hit the headlines.

As a result, people had started noticing what were, before then, self-published books.

As their popularity grew, and a cult evolved around Ironbones, Karen turned down offers from publishers who had rejected her throughout her career.

She went it alone for the first six novels, self-publishing. But she'd had a team helping her out for a while; assistants. She had the money to pay people, now.

The novels had been a huge hit:

Ironbones: The First Cut

Ironbones: God of Carnage

Ironbones: Blood Will Be Everywhere

Ironbones: Reign of Terror

Ironbones: Savage Night

Ironbones: 666

They had brought horror into the mainstream, and not just gentle horror, not just the safe kind of Stephen King horror—extreme horror. Unfettered horror. Amoral horror, some called it.

Now, with a seventh novel—Ironbones: The Seven Seals—about to be published, and likely to rake in the cash, more critics were bound to speak out—and more blood would be spilled.

This novel was also the first to be published traditionally. Karen had struck a deal with a small, independent press called Martells.

This would make them huge. Make them a target for a takeover. Make them a lot of dosh.

But they were a good bunch. Three college mates who'd been fans of the Ironbones books ever since the first one hit the shops.

Karen knew them from the fantasy/horror/sci-fi fiction circuit and found them enthusiastic.

So she'd offered them Ironbones: The Seven Seals cheaply. She knew she'd line her pockets once the book was published, so the paltry sum they paid for the privilege of publishing it was merely symbolic.

She enjoyed doing them a favour, enjoyed having them worship her—and her monstrous creation.

For Drake, however, it had all been demoralising.

He lost the job he loved, won the woman he loved. But was that reward enough?

He now acted as her manager. She paid him a salary. He was staff and it was demeaning. He felt no better than a serf sometimes.

And having a professional relationship with the person you shared a bed with wasn't always easy.

She was volatile, and hugely protective of Ironbones. Sometimes it seemed as if he were a real person, and Drake often thought there were three people in the relationship.

If it came to a straight fight, though, he would lose. Karen would always choose Ironbones.

She came out of the shower wrapped in a towel. With another, she was drying her dark hair, which now ran down her back. She was getting ready for a Q&A with a fan club in Dartford, just a 30-minute drive from the hotel. She looked at Drake. He was pale.

"Who's dead now?" she asked.

Kerri Joyner was the third woman killed by "Son of Ironbones", as the Press had dubbed the killer.

Stupid, Karen thought. Hacks were so desperate for soundbites, for tags.

Joyner was the wife of a Baptist minister, a forty-three-year-old mother of three and part-time book critic who ran a blog called Read Write—a play on "read right"; how fucking clever.

It tried to encourage young people to make good choices when selecting books to read, and Joyner advocated tomes that were "moral".

Unfortunately, she decided to jump on the Ironbones bandwagon. Called for Kaz Payne, "birth mother of this barbarousness" to be prosecuted on public decency grounds. Urged parents to campaign for the books to be banned. Very much like Merson did. And look what happened to him? But people didn't seem to catch on.

Joyner went a step too far. Brought a civil action against Karen and called her out.

"Let the coward Kaz Payne meet me face to face and defend her violent, corrupt scribblings. If she was able to write it would be one thing, but she doesn't write—she types. Just types and types vile words because that's what the untalented do."

Joyner's car crashed on a country lane in Hertfordshire on during a rainstorm.

She was found disembowelled and nailed to a tree, her tongue cut out.

Animals had been at her too, so at first it was hard to tell what damage was caused by nature, and what was inflicted by the killer.

The coroner did establish that she had been nailed to the tree before death. And her tongue had also been removed while she was still alive.

Death had occurred due do blood loss and shock after she was gutted.

"She deserved to die," said a fat guy wearing an Ironbones T-shirt.

"No one deserves to die," Karen said.

"But Kaz," the fat guy said, "everyone knows it's risky to take a crack at you, or at Ironbones. He'll defend you. He'll rise up and take vengeance."

The guy was probably in his twenties, but the shaven head—a nod to Ironbones; it was a thing among fan boys—made his age difficult to guess.

He had a five o'clock shadow and was pale and pasty—evidence of too much time in front of his computer, not enough fresh air.

Doubtless due to sitting in his room reading Ironbones: The Seven Seals, which they were discussing at the events.

They were in a room above a pub in Dartford. They were the local Ironbones fan club. Called FURNACE OF FURY, a reference to the first book's line describing Ironbones's birth.

The room was crammed with nearly a hundred avid fans. Virtually all male, all aged between fifteen and forty, all overweight or in need of a good meal. And a wash. BO hung heavy in the air, leaching through the Lynx.

The few females—thirty per cent of the audience, maybe—were Karen clones from the past few years: short black hair, long black hair, different styles of make-up.

Posters of the book covered the walls. Copies of the books were piled on tables, ready to be signed and sold.

Drake was there, lurking at the back, as was Karen's assistants, Carey and Ellie, who would be taking the cash when the books were sold.

"Still, doesn't mean she deserved to die," Karen said.

"Tell us about the book," the host said, wanting to divert attention from the awkward and possibly controversial questions regarding the Ironbones murders.

Karen cleared her throat and began.

"The Seven Seals brings together Biblical prophecy and a seven-foot serial killer."

The crowd chuckled.

"After the events of book six, Ironbones: 666, where he was buried under molten lava by Gabriel Messenger"—some audience members actually booed—"archaeologists accidentally dig him up and the impact causes the Seven Seals, mentioned in the Book of Revelation, to be opened. So there's the white horse, the red horse, the black horse, the pale horse. Then the martyred come out to ask God when He will judge the world. Then we have earthquakes and the sun turning black. Then comes silence—before the judgment, so it's Gabriel Messenger versus demons versus Ironbones. It's the longest book so far, and the wildest."

The audience cheered enthusiastically.

Karen scanned the faces. She caught Drake at the back rolling his eyes.

Robert Gilchrist caught him doing it too. He was sitting at the back. He'd caught sight of Drake at the outset. Gilchrist felt a seething turmoil in his belly. Sweat drizzled from his hair, down his face and neck.

The people who were sitting next to him had moved, fanning their hands in front of their faces and wrinkling their noses.

Gilchrist hadn't washed in weeks, hadn't changed his clothes.

Why would he?

He rarely left his room. And the more his mother pestered him to do those things—wash, change his pants—the less likely he was to do them.

Watching Drake roll his eyes at Kaz Payne's statement made him bristle.

You're in my place, he thought as he glared at the former policeman. It's me who's supposed to be by her side, with her.

Drake, a failed policeman. Just like Messenger in the books. Messenger never vanquished Ironbones; Drake never caught the killer.

Failures, both of them. These handsome good-looking guys. Thinking they were better than everyone.

But it was the flawed, the damaged, the broken who were the true heroes.

The likes of Ironbones.

The likes of me, he thought.

He reached into the pocket of his Parka, took out the envelope. It had the word MOTHER written on it in red capital letters.

He would hand this one to her personally. He'd always sent them by post in the past. Like the first one he sent after he'd visited his wrath on George Ellis. He did the same after Merson too.

Sent Kaz a letter.

She never replied though. Never thanked him for protecting her, for defending her honour. Never sent him good wishes and gratitude. Never came to see him.

But she couldn't do that, could she. Wouldn't be able to show her appreciation—her love.

Because that would bring Drake and the police to his door.

It would bring everything to an end. He was her secret protector. The guardian of her name.

The audience burst into applause and cheers for some reason, and Gilchrist jerked, coming out of his head and back into the room.

A girl at the front said, "Kaz will now be signing copies of Ironbones: The Seven Seals, so form an orderly queue."

Some audience members had bought the book previously and had brought along their copies to be signed.

Others were buying it for the second time, a brand-new copy, with Kaz Payne's signature inside. The copy they'd bought before was dog-eared and read to bits. These were true fans, the true believers.

Karen was ambivalent. Didn't always enjoy meeting fans. They were weird. She wrote because she had to write. She published because, like every human, she craved praise and approval.

It was a gut thing.

They lined up—all the geeks and the loners and the stalkers with their copies. Karen wore her best smile to greet them.

"I've got signed copies of every single book," said a ginger-haired student who wanted his copy signed "to Alfie".

"I've been a fan from the very first book," a girl with purple hair said, asking for her copy to be signed "to Jen-Bea—with a hyphen."

"I've got all the books and I was there at the start," a fortysomething businessman with a black shirt and red tie said, asking for his copy to be made out to "Allan—two Ls".

They all did this. Competed to be No.1 fan. As she squiggled her Kaz Payne signature on book after book, she glanced up at Drake. He kept checking his watch. He was eyeing the audience suspiciously. Still hunting the killer. Once a copper always a copper. Just like Gabriel Messenger.

"I fell for him because he reminds me of the detective hero in my novels," Karen had told journalists during an interview soon after her relationship with Drake became public.

Keep your friends close but your enemies closer, she thought now as she watched him.

"It's me," said a voice, jerking her out of her thoughts.

She flinched, the man's odour assailing her nostrils. Her eyes watered.

"Hello," she managed before coughing.

He was in his forties. Pudgy. Soft pasty features. Bad skin. Greasy hair. She'd seen him before at these events—lots of times; him and his green Parka.

He put the book on the table and waited.

Karen said, "I'm sorry, can you tell me your name? Who do you want it made out to?"

"My name?" he said, looking her directly in the eye. "You know my name."

"I know your face, but I'm sorry, I don't remember your name."

He blushed. His teeth ground together.

Karen recognised anger. She looked towards Drake. He was on the phone.

The fan slapped an envelope on the table.

He said, "I am Offspring."

"Just another deluded nut," said Drake.

"We'll be the judge of that," said Detective Inspector Patty Fry.

She was a short, blonde, fortysomething, lesbian. She had replaced Drake when he was forced to quit. Previously she'd been an inspector in another division. There was little love lost between she and her predecessor.

"We looked at him," said Drake. "His name's Robert Gilchrist. Loser."

"Maybe you didn't look hard enough."

They were outside the venue. Karen was still signing autographs inside. Her assistant had called the police when the fan lost it and started shouting that he would kill anyone who said a word against Ironbones or Kaz Payne. He'd claimed to be Ironbones's blood brother.

Officers were quickly on the scene and hauled him off after Drake had apprehended him and pinned him to the floor.

Now Drake was angry. "Making headway are you, Fry? Closer to catching him than we were?"

"I think so."

"So what new information do you have?"

"I can't divulge that to a member of the public. Mr Drake."

"You've got nothing. You're going around in circles just like we were."

"We'll be taking a closer look at your girlfriend, I can tell you that."

"You think we didn't take a close look at her? That I didn't?"

"I know you looked at her, Drake. Looked at her a lot. But not in the right way."

"Might make a complaint against you, Fry."

She strolled off. "Go ahead. Waste police time. I'm busy now. Got to question a suspect."

Drake watched her get in the passenger seat of a car. The vehicle sped off.

He shuddered and looked up at the night sky. Pitch black, no stars. He went back inside.

Robert Gilchrist walked out of Dartford Police Station at 3:00 am. Outside, it was wet, cold. The rain had stopped but the streets were damp, puddles everywhere. The air smelled musty.

Gilchrist tightened the Parka around his face.

How was he going to get home?

The police detective told him they weren't a hotel, so fuck off, pal, when he asked if he could stay the night in the cell.

They'd questioned him, but he told them nothing. He was trained to withstand any interrogation techniques the authorities used against him. Nothing or no one could break him.

He looked up and down the road nervously. Licked his lips and shivered.

He'd faced a lot of "where were you?" questions and queries about his obsession with violence, the letters he'd written.

He'd not said a thing. Stared the copper out. Showed her what he was, what she was dealing with. Showed her how tough he was to break down. How rare among men. How dangerous, too, if it came to it. And she knew—she could smell the menace coming off him.

Eventually they had to let him go. They had nothing on him. And they were scared of him too.

He started to shake, standing outside the police station in the cold, not knowing how he was going to get back to London.

Then, a black car came around the corner and crawled towards him, headlights on full beam.

Patsy Fry watched from the third-floor window as Robert Gilchrist shivered on the pavement outside.

He was a pathetic sight. A sad little man, as demonstrated by his complete breakdown in the interview room.

The duty solicitor had to help the blubbering wreck off the floor, and he'd given alibis for every single murder.

The letters he'd written were clearly cries for help, attention-seeking.

He was neither capable nor culpable of murder.

Fry shook her head, cursing herself, cursing Gilchrist, cursing Drake too. Of course he had done his job. He was a good cop. Hard for her to admit that, but facts are facts. He had, however, tossed his career down the toilet by having an affair with that writer.

She tutted and turned away from the window. Didn't see the black Merc stop right in front of Gilchrist in the street below, the door open.

"Get in," Karen told him from the back seat.

He peered in and gasped.

"Get in, Gilchrist."

He got in, shut the door.

Karen said nothing.

The car drove off.

THE FURNACE

RUMOURS THAT KAREN had bought the hotel where she wrote the first book were untrue. It would've been a poor investment.

But the room, however, was always available to her. She paid a monthly fee directly to the manager—cash in an envelope.

No one else could book it:

ROOM CLOSED FOR REFURBISHMENT

said the sign on the door—all the time.

Karen didn't want others traipsing around in it. The room was holy ground after all, a sacred place.

It was the furnace where Ironbones had been born.

It was where she had written all her Ironbones books apart from the second one. But when she had the money, she returned. Made arrangements with management.

The hotel had been spruced up since she'd first stayed here a few years back. A lick of paint. New carpets.

But those refinements were now starting to peel and fray. It would soon be back in the state of disrepair it was in when

Karen was holed up here, writing that very first Ironbones book.

It was where she had walked along the corridor packed with human remains—a charnel house.

It was where the world of Ironbones existed, a world that ran parallel with this one.

It was where she had found the door into his world, opened it and led him into her world.

Gilchrist looked utterly confused when she took him up to the room. Probably a virgin, his mind likely took a turn when he was alone with a woman.

He gawked, looking around the room.

It was gloomy and stifling. Smelled old. Smelled of burning flesh. Painted a deep, dark red. Stains on the carpet. Single bed. Small desk and chair. There was a pile of paper, and a pen, on the desk.

A huge cut-out of Ironbones stood in the corner.

Gilchrist stared at it, unable to move.

"This is where he was born," she said to him.

He was speechless.

"Do you want to meet him?"

Gilchrist looked at her, shocked.

Karen smiled.

"He's here, Robert. Isn't he?"

"What?"

"Is it you?"

"Eh?"

She pulled the scrunched-up letter from her pocket.

"It's what you say in the letter, Robert."

He knitted his brow. Said nothing.

Karen again: "We don't like people who lie."

"W-we?"

"Yes—we. Don't like liars."

"N-not lying, M-Miss Payne."

"But you claim to be Ironbones."

"No... no."

"You claim to have killed all those people."

He mumbled something. Was dribbling now, too. Shaking, looking baffled.

"Want to go home," he whined.

"Robert," she said, hand gently on his cheek.

He shivered: a woman's touch.

Karen again: "Robert, he wants a sacrifice."

He made a grunting noise. His face was chalk white. Eyes big and damp. Mouth agape, spit oozing down his chin.

"Wants blood, Robert. Wants fire. Wants roasted flesh." She gestured towards the chair. "Sit there."

Nervously, he took a seat.

Karen said, "I've written most of the books in that chair."

Gilchrist gasped as if he'd been touched by God.

"And now I want you to write, Robert."

"Me?"

"You."

"Write what?"

"Suicide notes."

After he was gone, Karen felt the energy drain out of her. She slumped on the bed, exhausted.

Her eyes were tired. She rubbed them. Yawned.

Something cast a shadow over her: something huge, wide, tall. She felt its presence.

Hands as large as skillets scooped her up into arms as powerful as oak trees. She curled up like a baby, pressed against a chest as strong and solid as a dam.

The odour emanating from the body she was pressed into was sweet, rotten, but pleasing to Karen.

The thing cradled her, rocked her.

"You will never die," she whispered, curled up, sucking her thumb.

"I love you," the thing cradling her said in a guttural, animal voice.

A little over twenty-four hours later, between about 8:30 am and 9:30 am, thirteen journalists from newspapers and TV stations across London opened an identical brown envelope addressed to them.

Like every journalist does, they started reading suspiciously, cynically, bored. But by the time they got to the second paragraph, they were hooked.

And then they all hit the phones excitedly.

DI Patty Fry was exhausted. So what was new?

She was sitting at her computer at Church Street police station. It was HQ for the long-running Ironbones murder inquiry.

Although the team conferenced at the Met in Scotland Yard, where they updated senior officers regularly, the investigators worked out of Church Street.

It had been seven, nearly eight, years, and they were no closer to solving the brutal killings.

It was depressing.

She'd wanted to be better than Drake. To beat him. Thought she could. He was just some flash harry, a media darling—handsome and cool, vacuous and vain.

But Ironbones wrecked his career.

And Fry thought at the time: I'll show them.

She didn't. She'd showed them nothing. And the top brass was getting skittish. Time for a change again, the rumour went. Kick Fry to the kerb, get someone else in.

But she wouldn't have it. Wouldn't let it happen without a fight. Without a hundred per cent effort, 24/7.

That's why she was knackered. That's why she didn't have a life. Hadn't had one since Clare left two years into Fry's new role.

Clare couldn't cope with the long hours, the bad moods, the "no, I'm too tired tonight".

Fry didn't blame her, but she was heartbroken. They'd been together a decade. Planned to get married once the government allowed same-sex couples to tie the knot.

But now Fry was single. Single and sad.

She yawned as she trawled through the evidence book on the computer screen for the zillionth time.

There was a kerfuffle. She didn't take much notice. Some of the lads were up on their feet, hurrying to the window.

There was swearing and there was: come and have a look at this.

And then someone said, "Fry, isn't he the fella you interviewed the other day?"

Fry went to the window. Looked down into the street. Saw Robert Gilchrist standing there, arms held out crucifix-style, blood drizzling from his slashed wrists.

He also looked wet—some kind of liquid pouring off him, pooling at his feet.

Pedestrians were giving him a wide berth, covering their noses.

TV crews were filming him. Photographers were taking pictures of him. Reporters were hurling questions at him.

One of the lads opened the window. The smell hit you straight away.

"Fucking petrol," someone said.

Then Gilchrist shouted, "DI Patty Fry, you did this to me. You bullied me. You intimidated me. I suffer mental health issues, but you didn't care. The papers know."

Fry's legs buckled.

Cops raced out of the station towards Gilchrist, but he held up his right arm. Blood still flowed. He'd sliced his wrists across. Not the most effective way to bleed yourself to death. But maybe he didn't want to die by exsanguination. He had a more spectacular end planned for himself.

The lighter in his right hand caught the sun, glinted.

The cops saw it and stopped dead.

Fry couldn't move. She felt sick.

Gilchrist lit the lighter.

He went whoosh and was engulfed in flames.

His screams stayed with Fry for a long, long time.

"I'm afraid, DI Fry, that we need a change," said the detective chief superintendent.

Fry stood in front of them: three men, two in uniform, one—the DCSI—in a suit. She felt like a schoolgirl being told off by teachers.

They had newspapers on the table in front of them. The newspapers had published a letter Gilchrist had sent them. He'd said Fry had been harassing him, bullying him. He said she'd accused him of being the Ironbones killer. That's why he was killing himself.

The last line said,

My life's not worth living because of DI Patty Fry.

She got the call a day after Gilchrist had burned himself to death: Come to Scotland Yard—now.

She went, expecting the worse. It wasn't even as good as that.

"We think you should consider your future, DI Fry," said the detective chief superintendent, "after you've seen the psychiatrist."

"And after that, if I consider my future to be with the Met, what should I do?"

"Consider it again, Patty. Your future isn't with the Met."

Patty Fry went home. She ran a bath. A hot one. A steam-filling-the-bathroom-like-a-thick-fog one. She got a razor blade and put it on the side of the bath.

She stripped off and started drinking Jack Daniels while listening to Bjork.

She turned the music way up. Drank half the bottle and was shit-faced as she staggered into the bathroom.

She got in the water. So relaxing. She took the razor blade. Cut herself properly—not like Robert Gilchrist had done.

Cut her arm lengthwise, from wrist to elbow. Slicing through arteries. Jesus, it hurt. She did both arms quickly. Stuck them under the hot water, which turned red.

Settled back in the water.

And died slowly, sweetly, solitary.

LIVE TV

Three years later...

KAREN WROTE IN THE hotel room. All seven books were selling by the bucket-load.

And now book eight was finished, ready to be emailed to Martells. It was called:

Ironbones: Legions of the Dead

It would be out in a few weeks and Karen was already well into book nine.

Her process involved sitting in the hotel room, in virtual darkness, battering away at her laptop. She would usually finish an 80,000-word first draft in eight-to-twelve weeks.

After finishing it, she took a week off. Spent time with Drake. In body if not in spirit, because her mind was elsewhere. In that hotel room with Ironbones.

After a week, she returned to the hotel and spent another month carving out a second draft, a cleaner one.

After another week's break, she'd be back again. Spend another month revising and rewriting, honing and chiselling, until she had a third draft.

It would then be proof-read, and Drake would read it. Say it's fine.

She'd then spend days without sleep going through it, tightening it, trimming it, perfecting it. Then it would be ready.

Book nine was going to be called:

Ironbones: Fallen King

and would tell the story of Gabriel Messenger's fall from grace, his resignation from the force after he'd failed to stop Ironbones's crusade of carnage.

Messenger would finally leave the light and turn to the darkness. It was, he would realize, the only way to defeat Ironbones.

Only evil could defeat evil; only rage could quell rage.

Karen stopped writing.

Checked her phone.

Nearly 7:00 pm.

She realised she was hungry and ordered Chinese food to be delivered.

She turned on the little transistor radio she always carried with her, managed to tune into a station.

She listened to music for a while before the news headlines came on.

The newsreader said, "A literary critic was murdered today in London after publishing a scathing review of the Ironbones novels by Kaz Payne, weeks before the publication of the eighth book. Guaranteed to be a massive hit, Ironbones: Legions of the Dead was lambasted by Daily Express critic Elizabeth Hathaway before its publication. She described Payne's books as atrocities. Hathaway, aged sixty, was found in her Richmond flat by her cleaner this morning. No further details were released by police."

Karen sat back in the chair. Switched off the radio. Shut her eyes. Pictured the slaughter.

Elizabeth Hathaway had been cut in half at the waist. Chopped to be honest. It had taken a few swings of a sharp implement to hack through muscle, bone, fat, and organ, according to the coroner.

Cliff Rogan wiped his glasses. They'd steamed up behind the mask he had to wear.

The upper half of Hathaway's body had been nailed to the wall by the wrists, tent pegs driven through the forearms.

The lower body had been placed in a sitting positioning on the balcony outside the critic's third-floor flat.

From below it looked like the lower half of a mannequin; it was naked. The remains had been tied to the balcony railings with wire to keep them in place. Blood dripped down into the street.

The critic's heart, liver, kidneys and stomach had been removed and placed in a Pyrex dish that stood on top of the oven. The oven itself was turned on to two-hundred degrees centigrade.

Rogan said, "Was he interrupted? Was he about to cook the organs?"

The coroner said, "It's just a sick joke, DI Rogan. I've seen enough Ironbones killings to know that."

Rogan felt sick. Sick at the sight of another brutal slaying. Sick that he, like Drake and Fry before him, would fail to catch the killer. He knew he'd fail.

There was DNA everywhere. Usually the victim's. It was almost impossible that the killer didn't leave some forensic evidence. But none was ever found.

The killer had spent a while at each murder scene, such as Hathaway's flat, where it seemed he was preparing to cook her organs. But despite that, he never left anything behind in terms of forensics.

Nothing but a slaughterhouse.

Sixteen dead now since the killings began with George Ellis's murder.

And the police were no closer to catching the murderer.

Not that Rogan really wanted to. Deep down, this killer scared him. Facing the murderer would be frightening. He was clearly more powerful normal men. An imposing figure, according to forensic scientists who had used studies of injuries and angles of blows to gauge the killer's physical attributes.

He was, according to evidence, more than seven-feet tall.

The same height as the fictional killer in Kaz Payne's—or Karen Davies's—books.

Rogan faced another sleepless night.

Maybe it was time to call on expert help.

Karen typed.

The newsreader said, "A church minister who described the work of author Kaz Payne as 'guided by the Devil's hand' was found dead today. Neville Gordon had organised events where the pages of Payne's Ironbones novels were glued together."

Karen thought, More idiots lining my pockets by actually buying the books.

She laughed; she typed.

Nearing the end of book nine, now.

The newsreader said, "It was only eight weeks ago that the critic Elizabeth Hathaway was brutally murdered —"

What other kind of murder is there? thought Karen.

"— in her London flat after she criticized Kaz Payne's work. As the murders linked to the novels escalate, Detective Inspector Cliff Rogan is urging members of the public to come forward with information."

She laughed; she typed.

That was funny, the cops asking for info from the plebs. Whenever they'd done that in the past, the nutters crawled out of their hovels. The likes of Gilchrist. Coming forward, claiming responsibility, making wild claims.

She stopped typing.

Gilchrist. A sacrifice. Willing to die for her, for Ironbones.

She looked at the cut-out of her creation.

Then back to it, typing away. The room darkened. It grew chillier. A shadow was cast. Karen shivered. Fear and excitement mixing. She felt a presence behind her. Something brushed her hair. A hand, huge and capable of crushing her skull. But it wasn't violent towards her. It was gentle. Caressing her hair, stroking it. She sensed a mouth at her ear, whispering.

"I love you," came the words, as if out of an abyss where they had been buried for a thousand years.

Without turning, Karen said, "I love you too."

"Who is she?" Karen asked.

Drake, sitting at the kitchen table, checked the A4 sheet.

"She's an MP. Back bencher. Seat in the Home Counties. Pro-morality campaigner—against abortion, against the pill, against anything she perceives to be a threat to moral decency. Big-time Catholic."

"You reckon I should do this?"

"Yes, good publicity," Drake said.

Karen narrowed her eyes. "Not like you to be so devil may care."

"What do you mean?"

She shrugged. Bit into another Digestive. Munching on the biscuit, she said, "You're usually averse to the 'all publicity is good publicity' line of thinking."

"What good has it done me?"

Again he scoped the A4 sheet containing information about the guests who were to appear on the Channel 4 talk show that would discuss censorship and violence.

Karen had been asked to be a guest. Most times, she'd be up for it. Nothing she liked better than a ruck with a hater or two. She was certainly willing to appear on this show too—until Drake backed her up. Then, doubt started to creep in. It wasn't like him at all. He'd always been against the sort of conflict these shows encouraged; the sort Karen enjoyed. Always urged her to refuse an invitation.

But not this time.

By now, their relationship was strained. He had not fully recovered from having to leave the police force. Being his girlfriend's lackey wasn't what he had planned when he joined the cops twenty years before.

He was a high-flyer, a cop on the fast-track to high office.

Until he met Karen.

Until he faced Ironbones.

Karen thought: All men come second best to Ironbones.

And she could see right through them too. Her partner was lying. He was up to something. She'd seen it in his eyes. But wouldn't call him out on it. Not yet. Whatever happened, would happen.

"It's just cheap, nasty, badly written drivel," Mary Evans said. "Dross of the highest order. Corrupt and vile. A celebration of what is worst in humanity."

A few in the audience cheered. Others booed. Karen smiled.

"Kaz Payne," the presenter said, "you're laughing."

"I've heard it all before from these fuddy-duddies who've never actually read my books."

"I've read them," Evans said. "They made me vomit."

Karen was momentarily stunned. Her opponents never read her books. Was this woman lying?

She glanced at Drake, standing off camera. Why had he gotten her into this? He looked at her for a second, something dark in his eyes, then he turned away.

Karen's belly squirmed.

The presenter said, “Do you want to respond, Kaz?”

Karen said nothing—she was waiting for Kaz to respond, whoever Kaz was.

“Kaz?” the presenter said.

Then Karen realized—I’m Kaz.

She came to life.

Just as Mary Evans guffawed spitefully.

“You have a problem, Mary?” Karen said.

“Yes, with your dreadful books.”

“I have a problem with your dreadful religion, too.”

Evans looked taken aback.

Karen went on:

“It allows its priests to abuse children, so you’re basically supporting a system that advocates raping kids.”

“Don’t be ridic—”

“And you’re willing to let young women suffer and die because you oppose birth-control, and a woman’s right to do what she likes with her own body.”

“You can’t compare—”

“You believe made-up stuff that kills millions,” Karen said.

You could see the excitement in the presenter’s eyes. This was TV gold.

Mary Evans sat back in her chair, eyes wide, her jaw in her lap, face red.

Karen had given her enough rope. Now she waited.

Evans said, “You disgusting slut—”

Karen laughed.

“How dare you compare your tawdry little fictions to a magisterial faith and a holy empire stretching back to the days of Christ; a faith that has saved millions of souls from hardship and poverty.”

"Oh fuck off, you old witch."

A gasp went through the TV studio. The floor manager made a cut-throat gesture. The presenter leapt in.

"I have to apologise for the language there, we'll go to a break."

"We're off, and we're back in three minutes," the floor manager said.

The presenter got to her feet, said to Karen, "Curb your language but not your temper, Kaz." She gave a wink and a smile.

Evans was seething.

"This is outrageous," the MP said, getting out of her chair. "You allowed this-this-this woman a platform to abuse me and insult my faith. You'd never do that with a Muslim, would you. You'd be accused of Islamophobia. But you're happy to insult Christians."

"Now, Mary," said the presenter, "please calm down. I'm very sorry that you were sworn at, and I think Kaz will admit that she lost her temper."

"No I didn't," Karen said. "I was completely level-headed. Meant every word. She's an old witch and I want her to fuck off."

"What was that all about?" she asked Drake.

"What do you mean?"

They were in the green room. He was on his iPad, trawling through social media to check the response to Karen's outburst on live TV.

There'd been a meltdown.

Twitter storms. Facebook fights. Instagram earthquakes.

Her fans had rushed to her defence and started creating memes of Mary Evans as an old witch.

Right-wingers and Catholics had been ready with their abuse too, lambasting Karen, some threatening her with hell, others calling for her to be arrested for threatening behaviour.

Then the centre ground appealed for calm. Said both Karen and Evans were partly to blame. Expressed concern that the broadcaster had instigated the fight on purpose.

"I mean," she said, "why that look earlier on?"

"What look?"

"John, what's going on?"

"What's going on is that social media has kicked off," he said, back to his iPad.

She snatched it away from him, hurled it across the room.

Drake said, "What the fuck's the matter with you?"

"Are you setting me up?"

"Setting you up?"

"Look at me. Look me in the eye."

He did, said, "Right? And?"

"What's going on, John?"

His jaw twitched. His eyes darted side to side.

Karen smiled.

"You're such a shit liar, darling," she said.

He ran a hand through his hair; blew air out of his cheeks.

He said, "It's a sting operation."

Detective Inspector Cliff Rogan, at midnight, sat in a parked Skoda Octavia in the small hamlet of Childwickbury, north of St Albans in Hertfordshire.

With him in the car, a driver and a detective sergeant.

Other police units were parked on the street, including a pair of Armed Response Vehicles packed with authorised firearms officers.

The car radio crackled. Rogan picked it up, said, "Go ahead."

"Bo Peep two minutes away," said a voice.

They sat in silence for two minutes. Rogan tried to meditate. Focusing on his breathing. His wife had introduced him to the practice. Or tried to. He just couldn't get going with it, his mind always drifting.

"That's normal," his wife said, "then you just bring it back to your breath."

Never worked, though. Too much stress in Rogan's life. But he was trying his best, and now, took a deep breath, following it all the way through his nostrils, down his throat, into his—

"Here she is, boss," the DS in the back said.

Rogan jerked. A silver BMW glided into view and turned left into Mary Evans's drive.

The MP had been a willing participant in the sting operation. Her husband was reluctant, however. He didn't want to put his wife in harm's way.

But Rogan had guaranteed her safety. Something in the cop's belly right now made him regret making such a promise.

But what choice did he have?

Something had to be done to catch this serial killer who had more or less put a stop to free speech when it came to Kaz Payne—or Karen Davies.

Firearms officers clad in black slipped out of the ARVs and moved towards the entrance to Evans's drive.

There had been no activity at all in the four hours Rogan had sat in the Skoda. Nothing suspicious. No strange looking seven-footers wielding sickles.

The garden had been checked out by the dog team, and there were two uniforms lurking along the path that ran along the rear of the property.

But whoever thought coming in from the back was a good idea would be in for a surprise. They'd have to scramble over a ten-foot high brick wall and two ranks of conifers, fifteen-feet tall.

An alarm system was also installed. So anyone trying to break and enter would set off all kinds of alerts and a "suspect on premises" call would reach the police before the invader would have time to clean his pants.

For the moment, though, it was dead quiet in Childwickbury.

Part of Rogan wanted it to stay like that. He didn't fancy coming face to face with a killer like this.

The perpetrator had become mythic. All sorts of stories were told about him. Tales of his power, his invincibility, were legendary. He was a scary fable to make sure kids behaved.

It seemed he, and the fictional character that had inspired him, had become one in many people's eyes. Shows the power of the written word, thought Rogan. And its dangers. People couldn't tell truth from fiction

And unlike the imaginary Ironbones, this murderer was so very true. The killings proved that. Rogan had seen the brutality. Seen it like Drake had seen it before him, like Fry had seen it.

And look what happened to them, his wife would say. He'd refused any therapy so far, but Mrs Rogan said he should consider it.

"After we've caught him," he'd say.

So the other part of him—the cop part—was tingling with excitement at the prospect of nailing this butcher.

And he prayed it would be someone who claimed that Karen Davies encouraged him to kill so he could nail that bitch too.

Jeremy Evans said, "I'll go in first."

His wife chuckled.

"Why are you laughing, Mary?"

"You are being brave."

"Some gratitude wouldn't go amiss."

He opened the door. She could smell his fear and silently berated him for his lack of faith, his lack of manliness.

But Jeremy had always been the weaker one. She'd worn the trousers from day one. Since they'd met at university all those decades ago, Mary Crestwell—as she was—had been the decisive one, the one to take the lead. While Jeremy scuttled at her heels like a nervous dog.

For him to suddenly play the brave husband protecting his wife was out of character, and ludicrous to boot.

"Is it because you don't believe in this nonsense?" she asked as he stepped inside. "Is that why you're so brave."

She followed him inside, and a cold sensation swept over her, chilling her to her marrow. It made her momentarily stop and think.

But then he said, "What do you mean?"

He switched on the light in the hallway.

Nothing happened. The couple remained in relative darkness, only shafts of moonlight strafing the entrance hall where they stood frozen.

Off to the right was one of the reception rooms. Jeremy looked towards it, nervous.

Mary huffed and shoved past her husband.

"You just need to change the bulb," she said and swung into the reception room.

The sickle sliced through the air and pierced her just behind the collar bone, sinking into her right lung.

She screamed at the sight of her assailant, a goliath swathed in tattoos and corded with muscles.

Her head swam as her killer said, "Mary, Mary, you have got such a big mouth."

With his free hand he drove his fingers into her jaw and wrenched it open.

And then he yanked.

Jeremy Evans raced into the room just in time to see the lower part of his wife's face snapped off.

Blood and gore cascaded down her pale blue suit and white blouse.

It looked as if she'd dribbled or stuffed her mouth with too much food. But Mary's table manners were exquisite. So this mess wasn't her fault. It was the fault of the monster who had just torn off her jaw.

Jeremy shrieked as his wife staggered, jawless, a sickle stuck in her right shoulder.

She flapped around like a living scarecrow. Blood poured from her mutilated face. It plastered her clothes and was now spattered all over the carpet as well.

Then Jeremy noticed the monster again. It had loomed forward, caught in the moon's flare. Its pale, dreadful face a twisted grimace, bearing sharp black teeth.

Its hand whipped out like a great eel snapping at a fish, and that giant hand grabbed Jeremy Evans around the throat.

The monster lifted the MPs husband off his feet. Evans was choking. He kicked out desperately. He clawed at the creature's iron-hard arm.

Then the beast hurled him across the room and sent him flying through the window.

"What the fuck was that?" Rogan said.

Radio silence was filled with a bombardment of voices. Missiles of panic fired into the peaceful static.

The detective inspector heard,

"Intruder. Man down."

Screams and sounds of chaos followed as the armed response unit rushed into the house.

Rogan leapt out of the car.

"Mary Evans is dead," Drake said. "Her husband was lucky. He was thrown out of a window. A few lacerations. Broken arm. Bruised windpipe. Three officers critically injured by... an assailant."

Karen was curled up in an armchair in the lounge. She was scribbling some notes on a yellow pad, ignoring her boyfriend.

He said, "Did you hear what I said?"

"I'm working, John."

He lunged, grabbed the pad and tossed it across the room. She stared at him. Got out of the chair. Strolled over to where the notebook had landed and picked it up. Returned to her chair and started to scribble again.

"Don't you fucking care, Karen?"

"You fucked up, John. You killed her."

"Me?"

"Your fucking sting operation."

"Not mine."

"You knew about it. You could have stopped it."

He slumped on the couch opposite Karen, said, "Why would I have stopped it?"

"To save Mary Evans's life."

She continued to take notes. He stared at her and said, "People die, and you just keep writing."

"Should I stop?"

"Stop writing this," he said, exasperated.

She fixed him with a stare loaded with loathing. Her chest felt congested with hate towards him in that moment. How could he demand that she stop doing the one thing that kept her alive?

She shook her head, infuriated, said, "Asking me not to write is like asking a sculptor to cut off their hands."

"I'm asking you to stop writing this... stuff. You can write something else. Something more worthwhile."

She let out a cynical laugh. Leapt to her feet, fanned her arms out as if to show him where he was—the lounge of a five-bedroomed house in Holland Park.

"This isn't worthwhile, is it?" she said. "This fucking house that I bought for us with my fucking money, the fucking money I made from"—she flapped the notebook around—"this stuff."

He shook his head and rubbed his face. Argument lost.

"I thought so," she said. "John, if you don't like it, you can fuck off."

"Seriously?"

She nodded firmly.

"You want me out?"

"Not what I said, John."

"But you'd put your books, your Ironbones books, ahead of us."

"My Ironbones books brought us together. They gave us this life. Without him, we'd be isolated, lonely people still struggling with life."

He looked at her, his brow creased. He said, "Are you serious?"

"Yes, I'm serious. When am I not bloody serious?"

"Never. You're never not serious," he said, shaking his head.

Karen's phone rang. She picked up. It was her lawyer. Her mouth opened. Her face grew pale.

"A fucking High Court injunction halting the publication of further Ironbones novels, and you have to hand over all letters and correspondence relating to your work," said the lawyer. "It's called an order for disclosure of documents before proceedings. The Court considers it to be likely that a potential party to proceedings has in their possession documents which are relevant to a claim."

Gripping the phone tightly, sweat running down her brow, Karen said, "Who's responsible for this?"

"Mary Evans's organisation The Faith and Family Movement. But they've been backed by friends and families of the killer's earlier victims."

Karen felt as if her head was about to explode. "Why do I have to suffer for someone else's crimes? This is utterly unfair."

"We'll be in court tomorrow, Karen. We'll get this overturned. But in the meantime, prepare all your documents. Get them ready."

"Why, if you're going to get it overturned?"

There was a pause before the lawyer said, "You never know."

Karen ended the call. Drake was sitting down, looking at her.

"Bad news?" he said.

She glared at him. "Bet you're pleased."

"What's happened?"

She was up, packing her handbag. "Bastards are trying to shut him up, John."

"Shut him up?"

"Trying to lock him away."

"Lock who away, Karen?"

"You know who. Him. Ironbones. People like you. Messenger. All those—"

"Messenger?"

They were staring at each other. Not moving. They were both thinking about what to say next. As if a line had been crossed and no amount of back-peddling would get them back to where they were. A point of no return had been reached.

Drake said, "You think he's real, don't you?"

She went back to her packing—avoidance in action.

"Of course I do. I'm an author. I have to think my characters are real."

"No, you named Messenger among real life people. Me. You think we're one and the same."

She said nothing. Sat down, put her face in her hands. Her head hurt and she was parched. It was as if the room was pressing in on her. Like that scene in Star Wars when Han, Leia, Chewbacca and Luke were trapped in the rubbish dispenser.

"Why are you with me?" said Drake.

She looked at him and studied his face, and for a moment she forgot that he was a real man who'd rolled around naked with her. She forgot his real name, and the name that came to her in that moment was

Gabriel Messenger.

Keep your enemies close, she thought.

Middle of the night, and she ferried piles of paperwork out into the back garden and tossed them into the oil drum.

The flames chewed up everything. Turned all of it black, made it ashes.

Karen stood staring at the blaze, a desire to dive into the fire and salvage her work pulsing through her.

But the little sanity that remained, the tiny bit of her that knew how to survive, an ancient thing that would be the last bit to go, kept her from the conflagration.

She couldn't cry because it was too hot. Her face felt as if it were blistering. Too close to the flames, she thought.

But she had to be there to watch her work turn to cinders.

She'd kept copies of her novels on flash drives, but all the hard copies—right from the early days of her efforts—were being thrown on the fire.

Black smoke stained the dark sky above London. Within the carbon, her words, her imagination, her creativity. Her vision. Now being spread across the world in tiny particles.

She looked up and tears filled her eyes. They watered because of the smoke. They watered because of the loss.

But at least it was a freedom of sorts for her dreams. Like a cremation. Hindus believe that life is made of five elements:

air, water, earth, sky, and fire;

fire being the last, and cremation was the final act encompassing all these elements.

Let the world burn, she thought.

They would suffer, all of them. The blood would escalate. The cruelty would intensify. The love would rage, rage, rage.

She was protected. She was defended. She felt powerful arms embrace her from behind and she leaned into a body that felt like the earth itself—solid, vast.

"I love you to death," it whispered into her ear.

Karen was watching TV, taking a break from writing. She was eating a peanut butter sandwich and drinking tea.

Drake came in, said, "Jesus, you're a stupid cow—you burned the bloody lot."

She grabbed the remote and switched off the TV, fixed on Drake.

"You offered me no support during this injunction shit, John."

"That's bollocks."

"Not bollocks. I wanted you to be out there, shouting from the rooftops that this fucking case is a crime. It's denying me my freedom of expression."

"You're becoming disconnected from reality, Karen. You're becoming isolated."

She said nothing. Drake didn't know her. No one knew her. Only Ironbones. Only he could make her happy.

When she wrote, she thrived. She felt alive. Giving birth to him made her excited. It was a joy to sit down at her computer every day and create.

But then the world poked its nose in. People came to look and to ask questions and to doubt and to sneer.

She got up, went to leave the front room.
“You’re just going, are you?” he said.
“Yes, just going.”
“You don’t do yourself any favours, you know.”
“You didn’t do me any favours either.”
“I’m leaving you, Karen.”
She walked upstairs and said, “OK, fuck off and leave, then.”

ON AND ON

A year later...

KAREN THREW HERSELF into her work. This was going to be the last novel. The end of the Ironbones saga.

She felt emotional, and a few times she found herself crying while she wrote. It would be titled,

Ironbones: The Last Dance.

Ahead of her, beyond this book, was a great unknown when it came to Ironbones. How would she cope without him? Would she cope without him?

She didn't think so. And she was fuming—with the person now who was trying to take her creation away from her.

Drake.

All her fury was fixed on him. He, as her manager and former lover, had encouraged her to bring Ironbones to an end. The fans didn't want it. She didn't want it. Ironbones didn't want it, obviously.

Social media sizzled. Fans argued over why she had decided to bring such a successful series to a close. Readers railed against the decision. Critics hailed the revelation.

But all the while she was leading Ironbones to his death, she was thinking: Why should I?

Jack Reacher went on and on, after all. Why not Ironbones? He was taller and deadlier than Lee Child's creation.

She had come to the hotel to write the novel. Sat in the room for days, weeks, she had no idea how long. Her assistants came over with food and drink. She never let them in; took the shopping bag off them and shut the door in their faces.

Staring at the flickering computer screen, she lost track of time. Her fingers battered the keyboard. Words flooded the page, as if they were actually pouring directly from her, via the keys, into the Mac.

She barely read them. Just glanced. Saw them form.

What she was really seeing was the action she was describing—and seeing it vividly too. It was happening in this room—every slice of the sickle, every scream, every spray of blood.

She was typing the words,

"You're dead, Messenger, you're dead,"

and hearing Ironbones's guttural, animalistic voice uttering the words.

Karen imagined the scene:

Messenger trapping Ironbones in the cave system where he planned to destroy him.

The earlier novel, Ironbones: Fallen King, had depicted Messenger's demise. He left the police, left his life. Fled civilisation. Absconded to the north of England. A rural, isolated terrain.

But he'd gone rogue, turning his back on law and order, resorting to the laws of the jungle, violence for its own sake.

And he'd break all the rules in book ten as he pursued Ironbones—for the last time

All of this poured out of Karen.

And when she finished the first draft, culminating in Ironbones's death, she felt like a gutted animal, all her insides removed. She was an empty shell.

How dare they do this to me, she thought. How dare they do it to him.

"How dare they do it to you," she said.

And a pungent odour filled the hotel room. A familiar odour. One to her that was security and safety, sweet and delicious—the smell of its mother to a baby, a baby to its mother.

Smoke filled the room. And then heat.

She turned and he was there, monumental, in the smoke. A towering figure dominating the tiny space: Seven-feet two-inches tall, shaven-headed, rippling with muscles, coated in tattoos, eyes red, teeth—bared now in a smile—black onyx and sharp.

She rose and went to him and said, "I won't let you die."

She ran her hand down his belly—a snake painted there with three red tongues darting from its gaping jaw.

She tucked her fingers inside the leather belt and pulled, creating a little gap between the pants and the skin. She smelled him coming from down there—all his heat, all his mustiness, all his power. He was a super-male, an über-man.

And he was all over her now; his hands, huge hands, strong hands. Hand that could easily crush her bones. But they didn't. They skated down her slim frame and she gasped.

And she buried her head in his belly and he wrapped his oak-tree arms around her.

Drake watched his ex on the CCTV he'd installed in the hotel room.

He'd put the system in a few years ago. Not entirely trusting his then other half, and her involvement in the killings, Drake thought it better to keep an eye on her.

After their argument that night a year ago, he'd packed his bags and left.

But he'd only driven down the road to a flat he kept privately. That's where he stayed. Holed up like a hermit, holed up watching...

There, eating a packet of crisps, he had his feet on the console as he spied on Karen writhing semi naked on the floor of the grubby little hotel room—as if she were being screwed by someone. Again.

Her legs were open, her arms up and wide like she was embracing a lover. She bucked and writhed, imitating the sex act.

It was a regular occurrence.

Drake always found it arousing. He had an erection. Had he not been so suspicious he would have masturbated.

Had he not believed his former girlfriend was somehow involved in the killings that had haunted him for more than a decade, he would've gone back home and joined her.

Maybe wouldn't have been greeted with open arms—or legs—of course. But she might have been horny enough—for old time's sake an all that.

But this wasn't about their relationship anymore. Perhaps at the beginning it was. And he'd given up a career for Karen.

He quickly realized, however, that for all her passion in the bedroom, and the way they went at each other, something was amiss with this woman.

And if bringing her to book allowed him some kind of redemption, he would turn her in. He'd been allowed back in the fold. Been helping her out for a few months; administrative stuff, managing her. She hated all that, so she'd agreed to take him on. Handy for him, because he was determined to find the truth.

How involved was she? Did she know more than she let on? Was she completely fucked up?

The cop in him wouldn't go away. He had the genes. Drake would always be on the side of law and order. He'd always looking for a way to put a criminal behind bars.

And if Karen was that criminal, or knew him or her, then she'd go down too.

Drake been in contact with Cliff Rogan for a while. Before the Mary Evans debacle, in fact.

Rogan had reached out to him: help me.

Together, they'd set-up the Channel 4 interview. Mary Evans agreed to be extra bitchy. They knew Karen would crack. She did. And sadly, Mary Evans paid with her life. Rogan nearly lost his job. Another copper of the scrapheap because of Karen's creation.

He switched off the camera, suddenly feeling guilty about watching her. This wasn't the point of installing the CCTV system. It was to spy on her with regards the murders.

Or was it? He wasn't sure anymore. Her phone was also tapped, illegally, and had been for a couple of years.

But again, that hadn't yielded anything useful. Just dull conversations with journalists who asked the same questions over and over again.

Karen had no friends. She spoke to no one, it seemed, apart from Drake, a few reporters. She barely went out.

People she'd known years ago, before she was famous, regularly popped up in the press and on social media to drag up the past.

The girl Karen glassed, Connie Wishaw, was a regular on Facebook, Twitter and Instagram, posting every time a book came out.

She was a talking head—albeit a scarred one—and appeared often on morning TV, afternoon shows, and had even done a stint on Celebrity Big Brother, though when the contestants were asked to line each other up in order of fame, Connie came last.

Karen had burst out laughing at that. Drake didn't blame her. Connie was always "the victim of horror author Kaz Payne". It was how she sold herself. It was on her website, on every social media profile.

Drake was sometimes baffled as to why she was still alive if there was someone avenging wrongs done to Karen.

Perhaps Karen had already had her vengeance on Connie Wishaw—the poor woman had to live with her face, after all.

She'd lost her lucrative job in the City and survived on handouts and appearance money; she was psychologically fucked.

Drake shrugged. Vengeance like that didn't come with a sickle and evisceration.

BOOK ELEVEN

Nine months later...

DRAKE, FUMING, SAID, "I've just been on television telling everyone that you're done with Ironbones. Now this."

She ignored him. Fidgeted with something on her desk.

He went, "Karen?"

"I can't let him die," she said. "I made him. I miss him. I love him."

Drake rolled his eyes. "For God's sake, you're talking like that again. Talking as if he were real."

"He is to me. You only want him gone because he reminds you of your inadequacies."

"What?"

"Your failure to catch the killer. He's still out there, John. Whether you like it or not. He's not going to go away just because you want him to."

"I left all that behind. I left it behind for you."

"An then you left me."

"You kicked me out, you..." He tailed off, blew air out of his cheeks, ran a hand through his hair, which was now flecked with grey: getting on, Johnny boy, getting on. He said, "It was a long time ago, Karen, so let's not re-open old wounds."

"They never healed, John."

"You asked me back."

"To be my manager, not my boyfriend."

"That's what I'm doing—being your manager. But if you can't be my client, and be honest with me about what you're doing, it makes my job fucking hard, Karen."

They were quiet for a few moments. Pulling themselves together. Cooling off. Then she whipped open a drawer, pulled out a manuscript, thrust it at Drake.

"Read it," she said.

He stared at it, not wanting to touch it—as if she'd handed him the Holy Grail.

She shook it, said again, "Read it. It's called Ironbones: No Dominion."

"No, Karen, no."

"Yes, John, yes—book eleven. And I've started the next one, too."

Drake made an exasperated noise, shook his head. "You're making a fool out of me."

"Read it," Again, she shook the manuscript in his face.

He folded his arms, stubborn. Said, "Only if you let me read what you're supposed to be writing."

Drake had negotiated a deal for Karen with a major publisher: two books over four years, six-figure sum.

She'd publish under the name

Kaz Payne writing as

KAREN MESSENGER

That's right: Messenger. A nod to her Ironbones detective, Gabriel Messenger. Drake wondered why she was so keen to use her fictional DI's surname. She hated that character. He was Ironbones's nemesis.

He'd asked her, but she was non-committal, shrugging.

She had written a draft of the novel. It was a thriller. Called:

EDGE OF GLORY

Tale about a female PI named Glory Jones.

"We don't want anything as gory as Ironbones," the publishing director had said, chuckling nervously, "but we do want something as exciting—a page-turner."

Drake had said, "You'll get that, for sure."

Now sat in his office reading it—what you're supposed to be writing—he wasn't sure at all.

And a couple of hours later, after finishing the manuscript, he'd gone back to Karen's study, told her, "Bland, clichéd, predictable."

She said, "You read the Ironbones manuscript?"

"No, I didn't. I read Edge of Glory. What you're getting paid six-figures to write. This"—he held up the dog-eared manuscript, gave it a shake—"pile of bollocks. Full of holes. Inconsistent. Half-hearted, Karen. You're not concentrating.

You wrote that Ironbones thing instead, didn't you? You have a contractual obligation to complete this novel."

"I don't care about the contract. No more than I care about the characters in that crap."

"Crap is right. And the characters? Two-dimensional. Dull. Not like—"

"Ironbones."

"Gabriel Messenger."

"I loved Gabriel Messenger once. My hero. You were how I imagined him to be. But when we got together, I got to know you, and him—and reality didn't live up to the fantasy."

He shook his head, baffled.

She went on, fidgeting with her fingers, distant look in her eyes:

"What I'm saying is that my relationship with Messenger decayed. And I began a secret affair with his greatest enemy.

"Karen, you're losing your mind. I'm really concerned. I think you should see someone."

"I don't need anyone. I don't need you. I only need him."

"You're—"

"Think you should leave."

"Leave now or leave for good?"

She shrugged. "Either way. I don't give a shit."

"This is becoming unbearable."

"At least we're agreed on one thing."

"You really have lost the plot, Karen." He wheeled away, going to leave, said, "Get your head straight for The Last Dance book launch, at least."

HE'S ALIVE

Halloween, 10:15 pm...

AND THE DARKNESS moved and became alive.

Jane gasped. Feeling electricity surge through her. Things trilling and buzzing inside her; parts of her never used becoming alive, feeling all liquid inside.

She shuddered with excitement. Stared into the darkness. The darkness stared back.

Red eyes appeared in the umbra. Then, a face. Manifesting slowly—high up, forcing Jane to crane her neck. The visage forming almost from the blackness. A pale mask, long and bony. Tattoos painted across it—ancient languages; the words alive, being written there and then. A hairless scalp covered in scars and snake tattoos. And a smile, then—wide and malevolent; jet-black teeth, sharpened to points.

Jane gasped.

Now the body appeared—torso, arms, legs.

A mutilated mountain of muscle. Tattoos swarming like living things all over the pasty flesh. The veins throbbing, pulsing black blood through the goliath, now. It bunched its fists—massive fists, the size of rocks—and the word

LOVE

was tattooed on the right knuckles, and the word

RAGE

was tattooed on the left knuckles.

The thing wore a leather waistcoat, or vest as Americans would call it, and tattered denims.

The thing was...

Ironbones

He towered above Jane, stood behind his creator like the Colossus of Rhodes.

Kaz Payne said, "Jane, meet Ironbones."

Just about finding her voice, Jane said, "He's alive."

"Of course he is."

"So it's not the end."

"Not the end."

"He's so... real..."

"So very real."

Jane was still staring at Ironbones. Ironbones was staring Jane. Drooling now, still grinning. Tensing his muscles. Breathing slowly, long, long breaths.

"He died in the book, he got—"

"He did, but he's here now."

"I cried when you died," Jane said, addressing Ironbones, "when I thought it was forever."

"Do you think it's right to cry when a killer dies? Didn't he deserve to die? Wasn't that how it should end? Good triumphs?"

Jane could tell by Kaz's voice that she was teasing. She couldn't answer. She was tongue-tied, and she didn't really want to think about heavy stuff like good and evil.

All she wanted was a story—and some love to go with it.

And she did love Ironbones. Said it now, too:

"I love Ironbones."

Jane looked Ironbones in the eye. Her heart fluttered. "I love you."

"Or is it my stories that you love?"

"No, him." Yes, him—it had gone beyond writing, beyond fiction. She said, "Love you, Ironbones."

He made a noise like tectonic plates shifting; grinding and groaning.

"Would you kill for him, Jane?"

An out-of-the-blue question, Jane was gobsmacked.

She managed, "W-what?"

"Kill for the one you love. Ironbones would kill for me. Has done. True love is born of true rage."

Jane's eyes went to Kaz, now: killed for her? Was she saying that Ironbones was the actual murderer? A fictional character. She looked at him again: not so fictional, though. Standing here right in front of her.

She shook her head. Was this real? Was she dreaming? Was that an actor dressed up as Ironbones?

"Or maybe you'd die for him, Jane."

"D-die?"

"Someone has to die. Someone always dies. It's a sign of love, Jane, dying for someone. Don't you reckon? Sex and death and all that. Love. Rage."

"I've killed," Jane blurted out. "Before. I have. It's easy. Can again. For him. For you."

Ironbones moved towards her as if he were floating. Filled the room now. Loomed massively above Jane. Her legs just went. Her insides melted. Her heart thundered. Two words in her head, over and over:

Love. Rage.

Drake drove the BMW into the underground car park. The LED lighting illuminating the lot flickered. Bloody playing up again, he thought. Got to let maintenance know.

He parked the car. The place was relatively empty. Middle of the night so most of the office workers were tucked up in bed. Or drinking themselves into a stupor. Or committing adultery with a colleague.

He grabbed his briefcase, copy of The Times. Narrowed his eyes and looked in the backseat for his raincoat. He cursed silently. Reached into the dark, patted the seat.

Shit, he thought. Did I leave it in the suite?

After the launch party, he'd arranged to meet the publishing director who'd taken on Karen's novel, Edge of Glory.

They'd met at a hotel where the publishing director had seethed and said, "We need to see this novel, John."

"She's pushing through, I promise you."

"The outlay is huge on this."

"I know, very generous."

"Then be generous in return—get me the book."

"You'll have it in a month, guaranteed."

They were in the hotel bar. The publishing director had stood up, gathered her things. Looked at Drake and said, "I hope so. Now, I've booked a suite, will you join me?"

He did.

And now he smelled of her perfume. He tasted her mouth. He remembered being inside her. But couldn't for the life of him remember where he'd left his raincoat.

And it was pelting with rain. He lived in a block of flats a hundred metres down the road. Residents had the use of this car parking space. But on nights like this, you needed a raincoat, and an umbrella.

Drake cursed. Sighed and braced himself for a soaking. He locked the car, turned, got ready to head for the exit.

He stopped dead. A chill ran up from his belly to his chest, making him shudder.

A figure in silhouette stood on the ramp that led down into the car park. Lights from the streetlamps created a halo around the individual. Behind him or her, sheets of rain hammered down, splashing on the pavement, pouring down the slope into the garage.

"Who's that?" Drake called out, his voice echoing in the gloomy void.

He braced himself. He wasn't scared. He could look after himself if necessary.

But the first irrational thought that came to his head when he saw the figure was:

It's him.

But it couldn't be. Him wasn't real. Him was a figment of Karen's imagination. But him had strangely become real over the years—the other man in Drake's and Karen's relationship. The killer. Or was it the character?

Anyway, the figure standing on the ramp in the rain wasn't seven-feet tall. It was shorter than Drake. Bigger, maybe; fatter. But not tall. Not towering over everyone like Ironbones did.

Drake blew air out of his cheeks, braced for the rain, now. Not concerned about the stranger. He'd just shove past them if they tried to hinder his progress in any way. Smack them if they tried any funny stuff.

As he approached, though, his bravado waned a little.

The figure was still standing on the ramp. The rain pounded the pavements behind them. The streetlights up on the highway shimmered and cast a strange glow around the apparition.

Drake said, "You need any help, buddy?"

Like help moving out of my fucking way, he thought.

The figure said nothing.

Drake's chest tightened. He blew air out again. Blew out the stress. Walked towards the statue on the sloping ramp.

As he got closer, the figure became clearer. He guessed it was a she. Short, rotund, she—he'd stick with that for now—wore a big anorak-type coat.

Five yards away now. She still hadn't moved. And Drake saw her face. Chin first—jowly; then the nose—bulbous.

Her flesh was chalk white. Streaks of black make-up ran down her cheeks.

Drake stopped two yards away from her. She reeked of BO. Hadn't had a wash in ages from the smell.

He was taller than her and he looked down at her, feeling confident now. He could have just walked round her, gone on his way.

But he was up for a tussle. He was irritated. So if she wanted a fight she could have —

For a fatty, she was quicker than he thought possible. She lunged with her right hand. Something caught the light, glinting.

Drake's eyes popped as she appeared to punch him in the chest, drawing back her hand, to punch him again.

But this time he saw the knife.

And he felt dreadfully cold all of a sudden; cold and frightened. Panic gripping him.

She stabbed him again. Right in the chest again.

Her first attack had pierced his lung. This second one nicked the aorta, the body's main artery.

Drake gasped. Staggered backwards, dropping his stuff.

His attacker lunged again, stabbing him a third time, the blade slicing the artery this time.

Drake would be dead in minutes.

He tried to cry out. The world went hazy. His body felt so cold.

His killer said, "The dead should stay dead."

She came for him, and he desperately threw his hands up, but it was no defence. She hacked at them with the knife. Sliced off three fingers.

Drake cried out and dropped to his knees.

The woman plunged the knife into his face over and over as she said, "Fucking Gabriel fucking Messenger, fucking die, fucking die, die, die, Gabriel fucking Messenger..."

Six months later...

Karen smiled, averted her eyes, cocked her head, touched her hair, blushed a little.

The interviewer—male, young, good-looking—said, "Come on, Kaz, put us out of our misery. Aren't you going to answer the question? Richard on the line from Derby is waiting, we're all waiting."

Richard on the line from Derby was heard saying, "Please, Kaz, tell us."

Karen, as Kaz Payne, was appearing on a popular horror podcast. She was talking about the Ironbones saga, which had ended six months previously with the publication of Ironbones: The Last Dance.

But the beast had refused to stay dead.

Rumours spread like plague.

Fans infested social media and chatrooms with gossip and conspiracies.

There was so much to talk about, after all—the books, the murders, the trial...

Ironbones would never die. Literary creations never did. They were gods; immortal.

The podcast's handsome host went, "Put Richard and the rest of us out of our misery, Kaz"

She smiled at the young man, thought: I'm taking you to bed, later.

Then she said, "It's true, I have written another Ironbones story."

Richard on the line from Derby made a hooting noise that resulted in feedback.

The presenter said, "This is amazing, we have an exclusive."

"You do."

There'd been rumours of another story ever since the trial. Karen had given evidence. Wept copiously, said, "I'm only a writer. These murders have had a terrible affect on my mental health—and now I've lost the man I loved. A true friend."

The defence barrister had a number of tactics, one of which was to accuse Karen of not only inspiring the murders, but of perpetrating them.

Forensics pretty much dismissed those allegations as being virtually impossible. And Karen also had alibis. Plenty of them. She also had the judge's sympathy:

"Stop haranguing the witness, Mr Roebuck. Miss Davies is not on trial. She has suffered a traumatic loss."

Yes, she had. John Drake had been murdered. Stabbed twenty-one times in the chest, the face, the neck.

"The twenty-first victim of the so-called—and we say wrongly-gendered—'Son of Ironbones' killer," the prosecuting barrister had told the court. "The last killing in a deviously-plotted campaign by an obsessive fan who felt some sort of twisted affinity with a fictional character."

Karen attended court every day, listening to the evidence, watching the defendant.

Watching her very carefully, in fact.

The accused sat in the dock, head down, mumbling to herself, rocking back and forth. She had to be nudged by a court official every time she was asked a question because she never paid attention.

When she raised her head to respond, she surveyed the courtroom with wide-eyed terror—as if she were seeing it for the time; as if she had no idea where she was.

She probably didn't. The woman was mad. Off her head.

But after seeing what she'd seen, how could you be sane? After going through what she'd gone through, how could you still be rational?

Karen had to go into the witness box. She played the victim too. Said her livelihood was being threatened.

The defence barrister laid into her, accused her of being a pornographer, "creating disgusting filth to lure the sick into doing revolting things".

He sounded like the prosecutor Mervyn Griffith-Jones from the Lady Chatterley's Lover case in the 1960s when Britain's class divide was exposed.

Griffith-Jones asked if DH Lawrence's novel was the sort of book "you would wish your wife or servants to read".

This defence barrister was virtually the same—out of touch. He was trying to portray the defendant as sick, a poor, abused woman influenced by an evil witch to do unholy things.

The accused had pleaded guilty to John Drake's murder. She was caught at the scene drenched in his blood. And when CCTV footage came to light, it showed her stabbing him multiple times.

But then she was accused of the other Ironbones murders—all of them.

And after hours in a police interview room, she finally admitted she'd killed everyone, from George Ellis to John Drake.

She gave the police information about the crime scenes that only the killer would know.

When she was asked how she knew those details, she told detectives, "Ironbones told me."

She'd repeated the same line in court:

Ironbones told me.

There were gasps and giggles, the judge calling for order.

All the while, Karen sat calmly at the back knowing what Jane Cooper was telling the court was absolutely true:

Ironbones had told her.

Someone has to die. Someone always dies. It's a sign of love, Jane, dying for someone. Don't you reckon? Sex and death and all that. Love. Rage.

It's what Karen had told Jane that night the superfan came to see her. What she'd told her as Ironbones loomed large.

Love and rage, she thought. Beautiful love, beautiful rage. Pure emotions. Clean and bright and sharp. Honest and true.

Jane experienced those emotions, full on. Ironbones, a supernatural being forged in the furnace of Karen's imagination, raped her, took her virginity.

And she lost her mind.

"Someone has to die," Karen had told her. Then showed her John Drake's photograph. Showed her the newspaper cuttings of all the murders. Drilling all this stuff into Jane's brain.

And Jane had said, "I'd die for Ironbones."

"Kill for Ironbones."

She did.

Truth was, Jane slaughtered two people. John Drake and Aaron James, the upstairs tenant. She was never charged with the latter's death. It remained unsolved. But she was going down for butchering Drake, and for the rest of the Ironbones killings.

Guilty of twenty-one killings. Pleaded diminished responsibility. The jury accepted that despite the prosecution wanting murder charges brought.

The judge said "Jane Cooper, I must sentence you for twenty-one brutal, sadistic, and obscene killings. You pleaded guilty to manslaughter on the grounds of diminished responsibility. The Crown did not accept those pleas. The jury, however, decided you were suffering from an abnormality of mental functioning which substantially impaired your responsibility for the killings. The psychiatrists who gave evidence all agreed. One of the doctors suggested you were acting out cruel fantasies that had been fuelled by your obsession with this fictional character, Ironbones, which you seem to think is a real person. Another doctor suggested you felt your actions were righteous, that you were taking vengeance against those who criticized both the fictional character and its creator. That you were unleashing rage in the name of love."

The judge went on, listing all twenty-one killings in detail. Then:

"Jane Cooper, for each of these killings, you will be detained at Her Majesty's Pleasure. I recommend that you should never be released—for society's good, and for your own. You will, however, serve a minimum term of thirty-five years. The Parole Board, thereafter, will decide when, if ever, you should be released. Again, I shall recommend that you should die in prison."

Gasps and shouts filled the court.

Karen had smiled.

"That must have been a terrifying period," the podcaster said.

Karen nodded. "Horrific. But finally, justice was served. The perpetrator is now behind bars."

"And screaming her head off night and day, according to reports, claiming Ironbones visits her, has sex with her."

"I'm not going to respond to tabloid gossip. Jane Cooper is a very sad person, a very sick person, who needs help. Of course we can condemn her for those killings and extend sympathy to the families of those victims. But I do hope she receives the support she needs."

"Do you think she should be released?"

"That's not for me to say."

"But surely you have—"

"No, I don't," she said.

He shuffled some papers. Smiled awkwardly. Said, "Let's move on and talk about the exclusive you gave us, then. The new Ironbones novel. What's it called?"

"Ironbones: No Dominion."

"Cool title."

Karen had pondered taking this guy to bed. Now she was changing her mind. She found him to be a prick.

"And when will it be published?" he asked.

"I've not decided. I'm resorting to self-publishing again. I want to control the process."

"Are you a control freak, Kaz?"

She smiled at him. Considered conjuring up the beast. Right here in the guy's front room-cum-studio. Have him slaughtered live on the internet.

There was no shutting him up, was there:

"You know, I really did think Ironbones was dead and buried."

"He was buried. But he's often been buried."

"You're right—under buildings, under water, under avalanches."

"And thought to have been dead too."

"That's right."

"But he always comes back. And he's come back again."

The guy chuckled. Bit nervous. Obviously sensed that his guest was getting cranky. He said: "The title invokes Dylan Thomas's poem 'And Death Shall Have No Dominion', I guess. And that kinda gives away the fact that he'll never die."

"That's right. He can't die. He'll never die. Only the unloved die."

He looked baffled, said: "Only the unloved—"

"—die, Messenger."

Outside the cave, thunder clapped. It was a furious noise, as if nature itself were protesting this travesty.

Sparks flew around the cage that held Ironbones. The electricity surged through the titanium bars. The charge crackled as it ripped through the cage, turning it into a flesh-melting torture chamber.

Ironbones gripped the bars, rattling them violently.

His hands smoked, turned black.

But he wasn't letting go. He was enduring the pain. Just letting the power tear through him, roast his insides.

Messenger scrambled away, smelling the flesh burn, feeling the heat coming off the cage, which was now almost engulfed in thick, white smoke.

There came one final cry of rage from the smoke—a last protest against death.

And silence fell. The cage dangled. Smoke encircled it. The chains creaked. The electricity still sparked through the titanium bars.

Messenger returned to the switch and killed the power.

He stared up at the cage, not quite believing what he'd achieved—he'd killed Ironbones.

"I've done it," he said. "I've killed you, you bastard. I've finally got rid of you."

Then the chains snapped. The cage plummeted. Messenger dived out of the way. The enclosure crashed to the ground. The impact felt like an earthquake, rock and titanium smashing into each other.

Neither giving an inch.

The cage sat there on the stony ground. The smoke started to clear.

Messenger held his breath, waiting to see Ironbones's remains—just a lump of molten carbon.

The ex-copper's eyes widened. His jaw dropped. He felt a chill run through his veins.

The cage was empty. The bars bent.

Impossible, he thought. Nothing living could bend those bars.

"I can," came the voice from behind him, as if the speaker had read Messenger's mind.

He wheeled around, knowing what he'd see.

Ironbones—his clothes charred, his skin blackened, flesh still smoking after being baked by the electricity charge.

The monster grinned at the detective.

Then he pounced. A blackened hand shot out, clutched Messenger by the jaw. The giant paw squeezed, and Messenger groaned, thinking his face was about to be crushed.

He could smell Ironbones's burnt flesh, and again he thought how it could possibly be that the monster was alive.

"I told you, Messenger. You'll never kill me. There's only one thing that can kill me, and you've never understood that. You should have—and then you'd have beaten me."

Messenger was retching. Ironbones's cooked flesh was making him sick. And the pain in his jaw was becoming unbearable. Unless he could pry open the monster's vice-like grip, he'd have no face—he'd be dead.

Then, much to the ex-detective's relief and surprise, Ironbones hurled him away. Sent him crashing against the cave wall.

It hurt, sure, but the pressure on Messenger's face was at least lifted. He could breathe again—for now.

He was certain that Ironbones would attack him again. Make things hard for him once more. So he took deep breaths, filling up his lungs, powering up his muscles for the battle ahead.

A battle he was certain to lose.

Ironbones glanced at the cage that had been his prison. The structure had been damaged by the electricity, by the fall. The monster grabbed one of the titanium bars. Shook it. Ripped it away from the rest of the cage. And he wielded it like a club, grinning his frightening grin.

"Time to die, Gabriel," he said.

Ironbones raised the metal bar and came for Messenger, who was lying on the cave floor, dazed, injured.

The former policeman's mind filled with all the times he'd thought he'd killed this beast. Too often to count, to be honest.

So many times he'd staggered away to nurse his wounds, leaving Ironbones buried under rubble, trapped under water, burning on a bonfire.

But he was always born again.

How had the monster survived? Messenger, after the first few resurrections, was exasperated.

Later he grew to accept that his efforts to destroy Ironbones had probably failed, and he'd warn colleagues, He'll be back, get ready.

The Met finally decided Messenger had lost his mind and let him go.

But he couldn't give up. His quest to kill Ironbones, end the creature's campaign of violent terror, intensified.

It wasn't until his research discovered the truth about Ironbones's birth that the secret to killing him became clear.

The creature spilled out of its warped mother's womb during a storm. Messenger had heard labour was induced when lightning struck the witch called Crone. Her child tore out of her, all teeth and claws, and she nearly murdered her offspring there and then. But she was too weak, the rumours said. The infant, a boy, grew quickly, and thrived on agony and suffering and dread. During his investigations—as cop and civilian—Messenger had failed to track down the mother.

"You wouldn't want to," the older generation who knew of her, said. "You think the child is horrifying? Be grateful Crone has gone to her caves."

She'd fled the asylum on the night of the storm after the institution caught fire, according to reports.

Messenger forgot Crone and devised a plan to kill Ironbones with the power that brought him into the world—electricity.

It had to be the answer. He had to gamble. Take a chance.

What other choice did he have?

Lying on the floor of the cave, cold, wet, wounded, Messenger now knew the answer to that question.

None—he had no choice. He had run out of ideas, of hope, of time.

"Kill me then, you fucker," he roared as Ironbones raised the titanium shaft.

"Slowly does it, Gabriel," Ironbones promised, "slowly and ever so painfully."

He swung the cage bar like a hammer. It smashed down on Messenger's left knee. Shattered the ex-cop's patella. Severed ligaments and tendons. Ripped cartilage. Splintered the tibia and fibula and snapped the femur in two.

White pain exploded in Messenger's head, and he shrieked, nearly passing out—but unfortunately didn't.

His head swam. He felt sick. The agony was blinding. Tears and spit ran down his face as he blubbered incoherently.

Ironbones laughed, said, "We've got to make them both look the same, don't we?"

He raised the bar, ready to smash Messenger's right knee, but then —

"Stupid boy."

Ironbones froze. His eyes widened. Messenger, through his pain, noted fear on the monster's face—fear for the first time.

"Stupid, stupid boy."

The voice was deep, guttural. Coming from behind Ironbones. From the deep, dark shadows, from the narrow, winding passageways of the cave system.

From the pit of Hell.

The voice gave Messenger goose bumps too, chilled his guts.

Ironbones cowered—actually cowered—and staggered away to reveal the source of his terror.

Messenger pushed himself back against the cave wall, as if he were trying to melt into the rock to get away from the vision of horror.

She—or it, really; it was an "it"—shuffled from one of the crevices in the cave wall. Clad in a black cowl that had crawling things all over it—insects and vermin Messenger wasn't able to name—the apparition pointed at a terrified Ironbones, and in that dreadful voice said, "Bad children must be punished."

Messenger's knee throbbed violently, although the pain had been momentarily numbed by the horror of what stood before him—the horror of Crone.

Ironbones's mother. The thing that bore him. The thing at whose tit he fed.

As Crone tilted its—"her" seemed unsuitable, too feminine—head to berate its child, its face was revealed beneath the hood. And its vileness caused Messenger's bladder to evacuate. He smelled his piss. Piss and blood.

Crone's skin was a blueish-white, and almost translucent. As on her cowl, things crawled under her flesh—bugs, multi-legged centipede-type creatures, worms.

Crone's nose was flat, just two large holes in the middle of the face. Things slithered in and out of the monstrous nostrils. Slug-like things, dreadful things. It was almost comical.

But there was nothing funny about this creature. Nothing funny about the sharp yellow teeth protruding from the wide mouth that went from under one ear to the other. A mouth wide enough to devour a man's head.

Crone pointed at her son now, said, "Time to come home, child," and as she pointed, her hands came into view—huge, like her son's, but with only three digits, thumb and two fingers.

Crone turned to Messenger and his intestines melted.

She said, "Then you will father me a new offspring."

Messenger screamed. He shat himself. The smell of shit and bone, now, filling the cave.

Crone slid towards Ironbones, left a trail of slime behind her, fluid from her sex.

The giant fell to its knees, blubbering, begging:

"Mama, no... Mama, no..."

His voice was child-like, high-pitched. A pre-pubescent boy's voice, begging his mother not to punish him.

Crone put her hand on Ironbones's scalp. Smoke rose from his head. The hiss of something hot on something cold could be heard. Ironbones shuddered, whimpered.

And started to shrivel.

Panting in terror, Messenger stared at the withering beast. The monster was shrinking, becoming smaller, degenerating, getting...

Younger, thought Messenger in a brief moment of clarity.

Ironbones was becoming a child again.

A skinny, scrawny teen now. Still bald headed, but with the face of an adolescent. The skin still crawling with tattoos, but the limbs not as muscular.

Then a toddler—tattooed, bald-headed, pale-skinned, but the mouth having hardly any teeth in it.

Then a baby, and becoming smaller and smaller, swaddled in the clothes he wore as a killer—the leather vest, the blood-stained jeans, the big boots.

The new-born infant writhed blindly, hopelessly, on the ground. Crone crouched above it, cooing, drooling. She scooped up her baby in one, ladle-like hand. Stood and faced Messenger, who was staring, hardly breathing.

"The child returns to its mother," she rasped. "Their love is stronger than your metal, all your weapons."

Then, to Messenger's horror, she brought the baby to her face. Her mouth opened wide. Saliva drizzled from the sharp teeth. A long, lizard-like tongue spooled out, wound itself around the infant—and drew the baby into the maw.

Messenger cried out. His instinct was to revile the killing of this child, any child. Even Ironbones. But his protest was sterile.

Crone ate her baby.

Crunched and munched on the fragile little figure.

Messenger screamed as the infant was mashed and torn in that terrible mouth.

Blood and gore spilled down its mother's chin.

Limbs were sheared from the torso. Innards were exposed. The tiny skull was sliced, and brain churned in the witch's orifice.

The child was pulverized, and Crone started to swallow it—and finally she was done.

She'd eaten her baby.

She grinned at Messenger, her mouth full of gore.

"Now we breed," she said.

Messenger shrieked. Tried to scrabble away. Pain tore through him. His leg was shattered and useless.

Crone came towards him. She seemed to get taller. Her legs stretched and Messenger saw them—getting longer.

She had become a digitigrade, a creature that walks on its toes. Like a dog, a cat. What had been her ankles were now set much higher, giving her legs the hooked appearance seen in canines, felines, pigs...

The cowl was too short to cover the hideous transformation.

The legs were thin, bony, white. As they lengthened, as the cowl rose up to expose them, unnameable creatures scuttled up the thighs, seeking the darkness beneath Crone's garment.

Messenger was drooling. His mind was melting. His reason was slowly disintegrating. Crone came towards him, a towering atrocity. She stood above him. Her drool rained down on him, spit and gore.

She said, "Fuck me," and lifted her cowl to show herself.

Messenger screeched till his voice box shattered.

JAMAIS VU

"—DIE? UNLOVED? I DON'T understand. Is he loved? Crone ate him," said the podcaster. "His own mother turned him back into a baby then made a meal of him, Kaz. We can believe that Ironbones can survive burning, drowning, shooting, crushing—a huge charge of electricity, even. But he was turned into a baby and eaten alive."

"Death can't kill a belief, can't kill love. People believe in Ironbones. Love him. It's like religion. He'll always live if people have faith."

"But, Kaz, things have to be logical within their own universes. We know Ironbones doesn't exist in real life"—Karen baulked, but the podcaster went on—"but he does on the page. And the world in which he exists is believable. But that world has rules and—"

"I make the rules," Karen snapped. He was irritating her now. An hour or so ago she was thinking of going to bed with him. Now she was thinking of smashing his face in with a broken bottle. She laughed to herself, thought of Connie. Then something crawled across her skin, giving her goose bumps.

The podcaster said, "You OK, Kaz? You've gone pale."

She said nothing.

The podcaster said, "For those of you listening on the internet, and not watching the stream, Kaz Payne is still with us, and—"

"I have to go, sorry."

She got up, shoved back the chair. The podcaster blustered, stuttered. But Karen was out of the door.

It was raining. It was dark. It was chilly.

Karen walked down the garden path, pushed open the gate, stepped out into the street. She stood still, shivered. Pulled her collar up. Tugged her hood down. Stared at the pavement. Rain pelted, creating tiny explosions.

She felt all of a sudden miserable, gloomy. She felt lost and useless. An "I've been here before" sensation overwhelmed her. She had flashbacks:

Come on, Kaz, writing's not a job, is it...

Images of her attack on Connie flashed into her head. She became dizzy. A voice whispered Love me. Karen clutched her breast, scared.

She staggered away from the podcaster's front gate, images again vivid in her mind. But not images from the past. Not déjà vu this time. The opposite: jamais vu, or "never seen".

She saw depictions of an attack—a knife plunging into a body, blood on a rain-spattered pavement, a body full of wounds.

She felt as if they were things she'd seen before but had the feeling they'd not yet occurred.

Nausea overwhelmed her. She could barely walk straight. Where was the car, her driver? She'd told him 10:00 pm but she'd left the podcast earlier than expected, just walked out.

And now she was trying to remember why?

Why had she stormed out?

Everything was blurry. The world was spinning. Her legs gave way and she fell on her backside on the wet pavement.

She sat there for a few seconds, trying to pull herself together, breathing.

She started to come to, feel better. Let the rain splash on her face. Let the cold air brush her skin.

She closed her eyes and breathed. She felt alone, at peace. Just her and the darkness. Nothing else—no critics, no Drake, no Messenger, no podcaster, no readers, no fans.

No Ironbones.

She opened her eyes.

They were walking down the road towards her. They were being soaked by the rain. The flickering streetlamps illuminated them, then cast them into shadow.

Two figures:

A towering man, bald headed, pale skin.

A tiny, stick of a creature in a cowl.

Karen, drenched now, her hair in rats tails over her face, gasped. Her guts churned. Her bladder felt heavy. Her heart raced. She wanted to run away.

Turn from the horror coming towards her, flee the fear. But she couldn't. She'd created this. Made it happen.

She had to face up to her demons.

Her legs felt weak, so she probably couldn't have run anyway. She leaned on a wall, looked around to see if there was anyone about. Anyone who could save her.

Messenger, she thought. Drake. Someone.

But there was no one. Just a few twitchy curtains. A suburban scene. Horror lurking behind the banality.

That word again.

Banality.

"I brought you back," she said.

And Ironbones looked away, sadness in his eyes.

"Look at me, I made you and—"

"Killed my child," said the hooded Crone, her voice guttural, weirdly male.

"I made you too," Karen said to the mother-thing.

She looked at Ironbones again. He wasn't making eye contact—staring off into the distance. Was that rain on his face, or tears? His cheeks, his brow, appeared knitted with pain.

Then Crone stabbed Karen.

She sucked in a breath, feeling a heavy blow to her stomach, cold steel chilling her guts.

Crone's breath stank, the rank air hissing out from beneath the cowl.

Crone yanked the knife upwards, slicing Karen up to her sternum.

She felt pain now—a surge of it through her body.

Cold liquid filled her throat, and she coughed up blood, started to shiver.

She looked at Ironbones, but he still wasn't looking at her.

"You can't play with your children's lives," Crone rasped. "You can't destroy without being destroyed yourself. You made me eat my baby."

And Crone thrust the knife deeper, slicing through organs and ligaments and tendons and muscle, shredding arteries.

Karen grabbed Crone's shoulders. Yanked down the hood. Tried to scream, but just couldn't, when she saw Crone's face:

Connie Wishaw's face.

Scarred, full of hate. Older than her years.

Everything became all of a sudden bright and all Karen could see was this white light, drowning out all the darkness, making her killer disappear.

And she sensed herself falling, plunging, wheeling...

"Mobile phone footage from three different sources showed you walking up to her and stabbing her with this weapon." The detective inspector patted the Integrity Evidence Bag containing the twelve-inch serrated dagger, drops of blood spattering the plastic container. "For the tape, I am indicating the knife discovered at the scene to Miss Wishaw. You followed her that night, then when she left the address where the recording took place, you approached her, and killed her. Didn't you, Connie."

Connie started to shake her head vigorously.

"Not me. Crone. Crone did it. You read the books? Blood and gore. Mother eating her baby. Crone was angry. Crone was furious. Karen Davies made Crone eat her baby. Crone killed Karen Davies. Not me. I didn't kill Karen Davies. Wasn't me."

"Connie, there's footage of you walking up to her. You're holding the knife. You are wearing these items" — the detective inspector patted the Integrity Evidence Bag containing a blood stained Ironbones T-shirt, a skirt, a pair of trainers – "when you were found, just a hundred-and-fifty yards from Karen's body. For the tape, I'm indicating clothing the suspect was found wearing when she was apprehended at 11:30 pm last night, the fifth of June. So, Connie, tell me why you stabbed her—"

"Not me. Crone. Wasn't me. Wasn't Connie. Was Crone. Was..."

"She's dribbling, rocking back and forth, off her head," the detective inspector said. "Solicitor put a stop to the interview. Wants a delay. Wants a doctor in."

Her superior, the detective chief superintendent, chewed his nail, knitted his brow, pondered for a few seconds, said, "We'll have to agree to that. Get a doctor in. Evaluate her. She might not be fit to stand trial."

"Unless it's an act."

The detective chief superintendent chewed his nail, knitted his brow, pondered for a few seconds, said nothing.

The detective inspector said, "She's fixated on these books."

The detective chief superintendent said, "Damned things. Caused no end of harm, those bloody books. All those murders committed by that Cooper woman, a fan of this dead writer. A fan of this bloody made-up killer. It's terrifying. Colleagues lost their jobs. Lost their bloody lives. Tell you what should happen, detective inspector, what should happen is that all those damn books should be gathered up in a pile, make a bonfire, burn them all. Like that teacher did. But a bigger fire this time. A blaze that would raze a city to the ground."

The detective chief superintendent paused. Felt the heat in his face. Glanced at the detective inspector, whose eyes were wide.

The detective chief superintendent reeled those thoughts he'd expressed back into the dark forests of his mind, said, "That's it. I'm going to put a statement out to that effect."

"That you want cities burned, sir?"

He grimaced, said, " No, no, books. Well... I'll temper it a bit. Say they continue to have a bloody legacy, even now claiming the author as a victim. The killer too. This one. Wishaw girl. Gone completely mad."

"Karen Davies assaulted her some years ago, so I think that maybe revenge is more of a motive than a book."

"She mentions this Crone, doesn't she, detective inspector?"

"She does, sir."

"And this Crone is in the books?"

"Apparently so, sir."

"There we go. Reason enough." He strode away, said. "Burn the bloody lot. Or words to that effect."

5:00 am, and the detective chief superintendent was going home. He'd go straight to bed. He was tired, having been woken up at 1:00 am to deal with the situation. But at least he was satisfied. He'd put out a statement around ninety minutes ago saying:

"These terrible books have now claimed another victim—the author herself..."

And he'd ranted about violence in the media corrupting society.

It worked a treat. It was all over the internet in minutes. The on-call press officer's phone didn't stopped ringing.

The detective chief superintendent said, "Tell them my statement speaks for itself, I won't be making any other comment until we either charge or release the person of interest."

He got to his Skoda, dug the keys out of his pocket. Yawned. Tried the fob. Nothing happened.

Then he remembered and cursed himself—he'd forgotten to change the fob's battery. His wife had been nagging him the previous night about it.

So he went to stick the key in the lock when someone said,

"The dead should stay dead."

He spun round.

"Do you believe that?" the figure—a small, thin creature wearing a cowl—asked in a strange, deep voice. "I don't. I think you can't kill things you create. They live on, don't they. Live on through love, through obsession. Live on and rejuvenate—reborn, if you like."

The detective chief superintendent wrinkled his nose at the odour of decay coming off the figure, said, "Who the hell are you?"

The figure slipped off the cowl. The face was pale, cracked, the blonde hair greasy, eyes red, lips blue, teeth yellow.

The detective chief superintendent's mind whirred and he found what he was looking for and said, "You... you're dead... the victim tonight."

"The dead..."

"The author."

"The mother"

"Mother?"

"Of this," said what looked like Karen Davies, and pointed above the detective chief superintendent's head.

He looked up, looked behind him. Pissed himself and made a strange, desperate sound.

The huge humanoid stood on the roof of the Skoda. Bald-headed, covered in tattoos, he wielded axes in both hands.

The giant said, "Hi," then swung the axes.

The blades sliced the detective chief superintendent's shoulders, shearing his collar bones, cutting away muscle and sinew, chopping into lungs, severing arteries.

The detective chief superintendent shrieked. Began to twitch violently. Began to make a strange, gurgling sound.

The woman who looked like Karen Davies step towards him. Said, "I love, I rage. Two things. Two pure things. I see everything so clearly. See it all in blood and in bone."

The axeman yanked his weapons out of the detective chief superintendent's body, and his torso started to fall apart.

But he was, unfortunately for him, still alive, and heard the woman who looked like Karen Davies say, "You can't kill love."

ABOUT THE AUTHOR

Thomas Emson is the author of eight horror novels, all published by Snowbooks. Foreign rights to his titles have sold to the U.S., to Turkey and to Italy. He has also published How To Write a Novel in 6 Months, a how-to guide for would-be novelists detailing the process he uses to write his books. He is married to the ghostwriter Marnie Summerfield Smith. He is represented by Mariam Keen at the Whispering Buffalo Literary Agency. You can contact him at thomasemson_info (at) yahoo (dot) co (dot) uk. He'd also be really pleased to chat to you on Twitter, @thomasemson.

Printed in Great Britain
by Amazon

39675517R00108